The Lost Diary of Anne Frank

A Historical Novel

Johnny Teague

The Lost Diary of Anne Frank

A Historical Novel

Addison & Highsmith

Addison & Highsmith Publishers

Las Vegas ◊ Chicago ◊ Palm Beach

Published in the United States of America by
Histria Books, a division of Histria LLC
7181 N. Hualapai Way
Las Vegas, NV 89166 USA
HistriaBooks.com

Addison & Highsmith is an imprint of Histria Books. Titles published under the imprints of Histria Books are distributed worldwide.

Library of Congress Control Number: 2020939374

ISBN 978-1-59211-055-1 (hardcover)
ISBN 978-1-59211-056-8 (softbound)
ISBN 978-1-59211-215-9 (eBook)

Table of Contents

Introduction

Arguably the most famous victim of the Holocaust was Annelies Marie Frank. We know her as Anne Frank. The exact date of her death is unknown, but eyewitnesses agreed that it happened sometime in February or March of 1945. Thus, February or March of 2020 marks the seventy-fifth anniversary of her death. It is hard to believe that this much time has passed. A young fifteen-year-old girl was caught in the grinder of a Nazi killing machine. She documented the trials of her family as well as her hopes of life beyond the war. She longed to be known, to be a famous writer and a renowned journalist. She wanted to make a difference in the world. She died in anonymity at the time of her death. Her dreams were never realized as far as she knew.

Prior to their capture, the discovery of her diary was feared because of the damage it would bring to her companions. Little did Anne know, her family friend, Miep Gies, had found the diary and immediately hid it away in her office desk hoping for a day when she could give it back to someone who would treasure it. The world has been changed by the rest of the story. The diary was returned to Anne's father, Otto Frank. With much gratitude and even more timidity, he opened it and began to read the heart and mind of a daughter he thought he knew. That diary touched him and he knew it would touch others, as it pulls back the curtain of evil to reveal the lives affected. Millions have read this diary, often looking around, fearing someone would catch them. Why? Because this is personal. People are not supposed to read another's diary. But this is what Anne longed for and wanted.

The diary has been read a multitude of times by many different people in many different places and in many different languages. It is safe to say that the experience of the vast majority of these was the same as they read the entry dated Tuesday, August 1, 1944, and turned the page ready for the next day. Great disappointment and sadness hit. The stark words, "Anne's diary ends here" stared up from the page. There was an emptiness in the pit of the stomach. The reader silently asked, "Is this it? What happened after this?" Anne had been so upfront in all her trials, why would she leave the biggest ones out? There was grief, wondering why she didn't take the diary with her? The answer is that the Nazis would have used it against them and their friends. Well, why didn't she start a new one and write of the next events? The answer is that they were not allowed to bring anything with them. Everything they owned was stripped from them until they stood stark naked. There would be no assets carried in. What they wore would be given to them, but even that would be taken away as they entered the gas chamber. If they were lucky enough to die before that, they were stripped naked, assets absconded by others, and then they were burned in the crematorium or buried in a pit. There would be no documentation allowed for a captive.

Even today, the questions gnaw at the reader. The last words of the diary, "Anne's diary ends here" are not acceptable. History records what happened. Anne recorded how it felt. That works well for her life before and during the Annex. The most important part of the journey is what lay ahead. The whole of the diary was heading to the climax, but just like that, the climax was not recorded. This is not how the modern mind wants things to end. Record a movie while away from home. Return home, sit down, hit play on the remote to find only the first hour and a half of the movie was recorded. Is the viewer content with that? No. Why? Because the viewer has no idea how it ends. That is where Anne Frank's diary puts the reader.

On the anniversary of her death, the facts are better known concerning what events happened after the Annex. What is missing is how Anne felt through these things, how she coped, and what her last thoughts and words were. All of that was lost. It was never allowed to be written. In this historical novel, anchored in the facts, *The Lost Diary of Anne Frank* seeks to bring a closure, to bring the reader to a proper, honorable ending. Let this tome serve as a credible conclusion to a life that accomplished all that she dreamed of and more.

Things To Know

Adolph Hitler and the Nazi regime drove their conquests across Europe, seeking to create a Thousand Year Reich. Their reign of terror would not last one thousand years, but it did last many more years than it should have. In their quest, a second goal emerged – to rid the world of Jews, Poles, Serbs, Russians, Gypsies, the handicapped, the weak, the sickly, Jehovah's Witnesses, homosexuals, and eventually Christians and any others who dared to object. The list grew ever longer at their whim. These were groups of people, but groups are made up of individuals.

Otto Frank and his family fell into one of these groups. They were Germans, but they were Jewish. As a smart businessman with an eye to current world events, Otto Frank could see what was coming. He moved his family to Amsterdam and started his business afresh there. As the Nazis began to see more success, he began to make plans to protect his family, should the worst ever come. He made a hiding place for his family and for a few others in the Annex of his company's office and warehouse. He hoped they would never need it. They would.

When the Germans invaded Holland, he knew it was just a matter of time. When the call-up came for his sixteen-year-old daughter Margot to report to a work camp, Mr. Frank knew it was time to make the move. In July of 1942, the Frank family moved into the Annex, along with another Jewish family, and later a dentist friend who was also Jewish.

Mr. Frank's youngest daughter, Anne, had been given a diary for her birthday prior to this and she began to record her life as she saw it. She would continue this practice into the family's hiding over the next two years. In this diary, Anne Frank addressed an imaginary friend she called "Kitty." She regularly referred to her entries as "letters." Her pet name for her father was "Pim." The family that moved in with them, she gave an alias name, "the Van Daans." Mrs. Van Daan called her husband "Putti", as Anne records. They had a son whom she called "Peter Van Daan" in her diary. To the dentist, she gave the name, "Mr. Dussel." Anne's best friend, whom she referenced throughout her diary, named Hanneli was given the nickname "Lies." Anne spelled the Annex in which they hid as "Annexe", and she referred to math as "maths."

Throughout the diary record, one can read of the feelings, emotions, and passions of a typical teenage girl. Exposed in this record was the fears and anxieties of being in hiding, being confined, doing without, the struggle to stay hidden, and dealing with the fears of being caught. Anne grows to love her father more, and at the same time to detest her mother increasingly. She grows weary of Mr. Dussel who shares a room with her. Though the Van Daans irritate her, she develops a crush on their teenage son, Peter.

It is known from the diary that there were many close-calls and mysteries occurring beneath their very feet. There were break-ins, scares, suspicious knocks on the walls, and concerns over the possibility of a fire starting in their building. Outside their building, the Nazis were arresting and carrying away Jewish friends from their streets and homes to concentration camps far away. The Annex residents were well-aware of what happened in these places. They feared that one day, this would be their lot too, leading most likely to death as it had for thousands before them.

Amidst all of this, Anne's diary abruptly ends on Tuesday, August 1, 1944. There was a three-day gap between the last entry and the day they were arrested. What follows is an attempt to fill the gaps from what happened next and how it happened to Anne's ultimate demise.

ARREST

Dearest Kitty,

The worst has happened. I am sitting in a holding cell at the Gestapo Headquarters. Oh Kitty, I am at a loss. I am at a loss because I no longer have you with me. I am at a loss because Father, Mother, and Margot are separated from me and perhaps from each other. I have no idea where Peter is or the Van Daans. I am even worried about Dussel. Where are you when I need you? You have always been here for me. You have listened to me. You have let me write to you my deepest feelings. Kitty it is because of you and God that I have been able to face the long years of isolation and loneliness. When I felt most misunderstood, when I had to put on the bright, cheery face during the day and cry myself to sleep at night , only you were there to hear my deepest woes. Where are you?

I want to tell you all that has happened; but before I do, I have to come up with some other way of communicating with you. I once took hold of the old adage *Auf wiederhoren* meaning "until we speak again" and changed it for us to "until we write again." But now, I cannot do that. They have come to our secret Annexe and have taken us away. Our worst of all fears is being realized. They took us and, unlike so many Jews before us, they did not even let us pack a bag. I had set aside my escape bag for such a time as this. I placed all the things that I just had to have in it – you first and foremost. But they emptied my escape bag on the floor and placed in it all the money, watches, and valuables they could find.

I wanted to plead for you but then I started to think what information they could gain from you. My diary told too much. After a break-in a few weeks ago when the burglars, police, or Gestapo were banging on the bookcase, seemingly to try to find our entrance, we huddled in one room and pondered what we should do if we got caught. I was very hurt when the adults suggested burning my diary because of all the condemning evidence it might hold. I told them then that if the diary goes, I go. Now I find myself praying you are not found, or that you are destroyed as just senseless drivel from a young girl.

We have each been interrogated. The Gestapo wants to know how many others are in hiding. They sweet-talked us with favors and then they threatened us with harm. They want to know who has helped us. They have arrested Mr. Kugler and Mr. Kleiman. I don't know about Miep or Bep or the others. Father told us before they took each of us to interrogate to say nothing, no matter what. Kitty, if they find you, they will have all they need. I pray God won't let them find you. I pray you are destroyed and that if we get out, I can remember and recreate you.

But now, that brings me to a big problem in my mind and heart. How can I make it without writing what I feel? How can I make it without having you, Kitty, who knows my innermost thoughts? It has taken me two days of sleepless nights to come up with an answer. I must stay focused. I must stay strong. I must also have some sort of inner peace. I prayed for an answer and it came to me this morning. *Auf wiederhoren.* Until we speak again. I don't have to write you, Kitty. Everything I have written you, I have thought before I wrote. Everything I have written you, I noticed, I even moved my lips as I wrote. What a relief! I can speak to you. I can still confide in you. I can still ask you questions and tell you secrets. The practice that has kept me sane these past two years can continue. Oh Kit. I can make it. You will listen. We are still connected. Despite our dire trouble, the war is still going well. The Allies are expected any day. The German soldiers look worried. They speak faster. They don't seem near as confident. If we make it through this, I pray I will be able to recall all I have shared with you so that I can write it all down again. I want to be a journalist. I want to be a famous writer who has documented all that has gone on and all that we have suffered. I still have that in me and it is still possible. Now I can sleep.

Yours, Anne M. Frank

Monday, August 7, 1944

Dearest Kitty,

It is morning. I made it through the night. I remember that I once lost my fountain pen. Do you remember ? I memorialized my thoughts for you and took another pen and kept writing. You didn't mind. Then I left my other pen in the attic for a day so I wrote to you in pencil. You did not object. Now, I have neither pen or pencil, nor paper, but I can still write to you in my heart through my emotions. I am relieved. I heard some screams during the night and a lot of weeping. Some of it was mine. I need to tell you how we got here. Friday, August 4th seemed like just another morning. I had come down from the attic after breathing in some fresh air. I had looked out at a cloudless, clear blue sky and enjoyed the beauty of nature for a few minutes. Father came up to Peter's room to help him with some school work. I left because I was still uneasy about him seeing us together. As I came down to join Mother and Margot, Miep came up to see us and get our grocery order. Mother gave her our list, which included paper for you, Kitty. You and I had run out of it a few days before. I greeted Miep the usual way, "Hello Miep, what's the news? " She was cheerful. We were getting great news on the war. The Germans were in a bloody, destructive retreat. The Allies were pushing forward. Churchill was confident as ever. He gives his nation great confidence. He gave us great confidence too. Things were changing. Sadly, our confidence would soon disappear. Miep left. The bookcase was closed. The day time routine of silence, no toilet flushes, and sock-feet walking resumed. It was just another day in our private prison of non-existence to the outside world. This would be our portion. Or so we thought.

There was a bang on the bookshelf. Our conversation dropped to a hush. We were petrified. For nights and nights, we had horrific dreams of this, dreams that we would not share with each other so as to not re-kindle our fear. I was afraid to even write them to you, Kitty, because the pen would not even stay still in my hand. We then heard Mr. Kugler's voice protesting. We heard the bookcase open, sounding like it was torn from its hinges, and then the running of many boots up our stairs. Mother grabbed Margot and me in a tight embrace, as if to shield or hide us. There before us, holding a gun cocked and ready for fire, was an SS guard and some Dutch policemen. One stayed with us, while the others began to rush through the room. Fearful, I assumed that the others might come under gunfire at any effort to resist. The Van Daans came down, saw, and immediately lifted their hands in the air. Mrs. Van Daan began to weep. Father and Peter followed. Father, in an authoritative voice that I haven't heard since we went into hiding, spoke to them as if he were addressing some of his warehouse employees. He assured them that the guns were not necessary. They escorted them beside us. Father wrapped his arms around Mother who was wrapped around Margot and me. I was trembling. Our teeth were chattering in fear. The day had come. They brought down Dussel. There we stood.

The SS guard introduced himself to us, SS-onderofficier Karl Silberbauer. I had not been up this close to an SS officer in many years. I had imagined many times what this officer would look like if we were found. He was nothing like I had imagined. He was firm, but respectful. He was clearly the chief officer. Since Father had been the spokesman and seemed to be the one in charge, Silberbauer addressed his questions to Pim. He asked, "Were there any others staying here?" Pim said, "No." He asked, "How long have you been hiding here?" Father answered, "Two years and one month." It was that answer that caused the SS officer to stand silent. He looked at the other officers, then at Kugler. He closed his eyes as if to do the maths, like I do when I am struggling with my homework. He asked again, "How long have you eight been hiding here?" Father answered again, "Two years and one month." The guard couldn't believe him. Father took him to the wall where he had been monitoring the war's progress. Then he pointed to the markings on the wall where he and mother had been marking our growth. Father called me to himself, and had me stand against the wall like I had so many times before. I felt like I was not standing to be measured now, but to be shot by the Nazi firing squad. I didn't want to do it, but Father assured me it would be okay. The man said to Father that he had a lovely daughter. That did not please me in the least. I did what they asked. The arresting officer looked at the markings, gently moved me to the side, and shook his head. I guess he believed Father. With that, he said, "You must come with us. Make no moves. Do not try to escape and do not say a word. All will be alright if you just do what I say." We all looked at Father. He nodded, and we followed Silberbauer down our steps. It was the first time we had ever walked these stairs with outsiders, and yet it seemed so familiar as we had replayed this scene in our minds for months and nights on end.

We walked by Miep. She was white as a sheet, and she was silent. She was filled with tears but let out not one whimper of goodbye. It took great effort to not acknowledge anyone there. They walked us outside in the broad daylight on a sunny morning. The fresh air was strangely invigorating. How wonderful this would be on some other occasion – to feel the breeze, to have the stench behind us, to hear the rustling of the leaves on the trees, to actually see the birds that were singing, to look up and see the whole of the sky with the clouds moving rather than through a rectangular restricted view. But this was not any other occasion. I thought this might be our last day on this earth. I strained to look at Peter. We had enjoyed many day dreams of being outside together. How was he holding up? Was he afraid? He had been so brave in the Annexe and in the warehouse. Every time a burglar penetrated our building, Peter had run to the danger. I was glad to see he seemed as brave the day of our arrest as he had been the days of our hiding. I noticed people on the streets watching us. They looked as if they were deeply sorry for us, but none of them were willing to say a word or raise a hand to help us. It had been this way ever since the Germans came into Holland. While everyone was criticizing Britain, as I have always said, there was enough blame to place on Holland as well. We had seen others hauled away who were not blessed enough to find a place to hide. Now it was our turn.

They loaded us single file into the truck, closed the door, and began driving us to our next destination. We sat across from each other with eyes wide open. Mrs. Van Daan laid her head on her "Putti." We wanted to speak, to discuss what was happening, how it happened, how they knew, and what would happen next, but we could not speak. We had the Dutch police on each side of us in the back of the truck. Father just motioned with his head, "silence." They escorted us into the Gestapo headquarters. It was a sharply painted building, almost sterile. Our steps echoed off the concrete floors and the heavily plastered walls. We passed by a big office. I peeked in. There on the wall was a picture of the Fuhrer, Hitler himself. He adorned many offices in many poses. His eyes glared with hatred, as if he was seeking to root out through his eyes every last Jew. If only you had been there, Kitty, and would have seen that face on the wall with all those men walking lock-step beneath, carrying out the will of a mad man.

They separated us and questioned us one by one. They used different techniques with each type of person. They seemed to reason with Father as an equal. They showed their power to Mother and Mrs. Van D. I believe their aim was to destroy the women's confidence by pushing them to betray all that was concealed. With me, they tried to intimidate. They threatened harm to my parents and my sister if I did not talk. I kept telling myself that I was no normal fifteen-year-old girl, dependent on Mother and Father. I was strong. I was independent. I could face this and overcome. That's what I tried to project on the outside, Kitty, but on the inside, I was shaking, doubting, and weeping. I was determined that those emotions would have to wait for my bunk.

The Nazi interrogator kept trying to get me to talk. He offered rewards and then punishment. If there were time for humor in all this, a paradox popped in my head. What a reversal from three years earlier! In class, Mr. Keesing called me a chatterbox. He would punish me with writing assignments to deter my incessant talking. Every time, I took the challenge and got the better of him. He finally let me talk all I wanted without scolding. If I could do that with Mr. Keesing for talking too much, I figured I could do it with these officers for not talking at all. Kit, how Mr. Keesing would have fainted seeing the day when I refused to talk! I don't know what I did, but like with Mr. Keesing, the guard must have admired my pluck and strength like Peter and Margot did. They let me go back to my cell. Now we wait. What will happen to us now? I am glad you are not here Kitty, and I hope they don't find you either, or we will all be in trouble.

Yours, Anne M. Frank

WESTERBORK

Dearest Kitty,

For over two years, you always knew where to find me. Now, I have moved for the third time in five days. I hope you can keep up. It's evening now. We are now in the dreaded Westerbork. Earlier today, they took us from the detention center and loaded us on passenger trains. We were a little surprised at our transportation, having heard so much about cattle cars. Maybe God was blessing us. As they loaded us in, I was one of the first into the passenger car, holding Pim's hand. I went straight to the seat by a window. Father was so kind to place his arm around me on one side and around Mother with the other. Margot sat right beside us on the other side of the aisle. We were crammed in. I was pressed against the window, but I didn't mind. I had a full view of the nature that I had so long missed. I hardly even looked at my family. They had been my only view for too long. I could not get over the life that passed outside that window. I could hardly grasp the fact that we were out of the Annexe. A great hope came over me as it always did when I looked at the blue sky, the trees, and the God-created beauty. I was in awe. I felt just a touch of freedom. It made me wonder why we stayed hidden for so long. I knew there may be terrible things ahead, but I just couldn't think of that at that moment. I had wished the train ride would never end. Heaven was touching earth right outside that window, and I was seeing it for what seemed like the first time.

When our train passed through the gate of Westerbork, it seemed much of what Miep had told us about this place was true. The camp is packed with people and there are electrified barbed wire fences all around us. But what Miep didn't know was, there was a kinder, gentler feel to this place. There is a school here, a restaurant, and even a hair-dresser. Of course, we have no access to any of these. We are in the punishment barracks because we had the audacity to hide from our captors and resist their call-ups. For this, it is our understanding that we have been assigned to hard labor to show us the error of our ways. There was extra food available for any who had money, but we had no money. We had all we owned taken from us or left in the Annexe. It is our understanding that the SS leaves much of the running of the place to a German Jewish committee. We are hoping this will be to our good.

When we unloaded the train and were led to our barracks, the men were assigned to their barracks for sleep, and the women led to theirs. Mother just hung on to Margot and me as we wept. I never really liked her affection or her embrace. I prefer to deal with this on my own as you know, but the inner Anne felt the need to let her and the outer Anne obliged. The truth be told, Kitty, for the first time in a long time, I was surprised how much I needed and even liked that hug. I was starting to see my Mother in a different light. Now, I have seen some good in her in the past, but it doesn't take long for the detestable part to surface. Maybe as I am changing, she is changing too.

A few of the women came to us tonight as they saw we were afraid, wide-eyed yet tear-filled. They came to comfort us and tell us that Westerbork won't be as bad as we fear. The labor is hard, but the best part is, we get to talk and visit as long as we do our work. In the evenings, we are able to get back together with our loved ones who are here and eat what food they give us, visit, fellowship, and regain a sense of normalcy. I have to admit my thoughts of normalcy are continents away from this, but I am trusting this is going to be fine. How I pray the Russians, or the British, or the Americans come soon. If so, we may have passed the worst part.

Yours, Anne M. Frank

Wednesday, August 9, 1944

Dearest Kitty,

I am glad to say we made it through our first day here. The work was hard and dusty. We are assigned to break up batteries all day. It is monotonous and surely cannot be healthy, but compared to being cooped up in an Annexe where we cannot flush the toilet, we have to sit in silence during the day, and deny ourselves an "outside" voice for days upon end; this is a welcomed change. I almost feel like we were hired by a war factory in northern Amsterdam. The only thing lacking is we do not clock in, though there is a roll call every day. Speaking of lacking, this place is not as bad as we feared from the start. The water supply is not that good, and the sanitary conditions leave much to be desired. I say that, but you know that our conditions were not that good in the Annexe either. This place is a whole lot worse for those who were taken from the streets of freedom. We had the, dare I say, privilege to warm up to such situations over the past few years.

Yours, Anne M. Frank

Thursday, August 10, 1944

Dearest Kitty,

You would be surprised how good the eight of us are getting along after our work is done. Even old Dussel isn't nearly as bad to look at. I no longer have to hear his snoring and gasping for breath. I don't have to put up with his restroom schedule, which I think Mussolini may have scheduled the Italian trains by. He does not seem near as stupid now that I am no longer living with him. The Van Daans are getting along glowingly. It seems their love is no longer forced. Father still has the lead in our family-of-eight gatherings. How I love Pim. I respect him more every day. I want to marry a man like Pim. He is the most humble man I have ever known. In this wider circle of men, he stands out all the taller. The men are staying together, and sleeping in the same bunk space. I sure hope Peter lets Father rub off on him. Mother is tolerable. I am amazed at the difference in her with so many other women to see and interact with. She seems to be in her element. She has a quieter, wiser look to her than I have ever seen. Now, don't get me wrong Kit, I still don't think of her as my mother. But as a woman, I see some enviable traits beginning to rise, especially with the backdrop of others.

Yours, Anne M. Frank

Friday, August 11, 1944

Dearest Kitty,

I need to visit with you about a huge mystery. The eight of us were able to delve into the subject a little this evening, now that we are getting our bearings in this new environment. The mystery is, who turned us in to the Gestapo? We have several suspects. This wanting an answer hits us hard when we think of Miep, Bep, Jan, Mr. Kugler, and Mr. Kleinman in particular. Here are all these people standing up for right in a world of wrong. They were willing to risk their lives to go against the grain of self-preservation for the sake of others. Where is our beloved, extended family now? These who shared our meals, shared our room, shared our fears – where are they? Are they alive? Are they in prison? Is their situation worse than ours? It breaks my heart. I pray that God will be with them, as He has been with us. I pray they will make it through this. Though I hope one day to get out of this, I am praying at the moment all the more for them to get out of it. They did nothing wrong, but to love the hated. They sacrificed everything for us. They did without so we could have. We did not have much, but we would have had nothing had it not been for them.

This brings me back to Father. What a good man, boss, and co-worker he must have been to these for them to risk everything for him and his family. I love Pim so much. The more I think of him, the more I grieve over that selfish letter I wrote to him concerning my independence and his failure as a Father. He acts as if I never wrote the letter. I act the same. But, I still remember the letter. When he says our prayers with us in the evening before we go to our separate barracks, I cannot help but want to cry when I think of the hurt I brought Pim. I pray he forgets and forgives as much as he seems to have. And, I pray that I will be as good as he is one day. God knows I am praying to be changed, and I am committed to being changed.

Yours, Anne M. Frank

Sunday, August 13, 1944

Dearest Kitty,

I bet you never thought I would be so faithful to speak to you once I lost my pen and paper. The truth is, Kitty, the more I face, the more I need to write or speak to you. I have a feeling of optimism. We still are hearing the aeroplanes at night. The bombings continue all around us. We just hope they don't hit this place where we are. From the sky, I am sure it looks like we are German sympathizers working in a war-making factory, an ideal target. If only those boys in those planes could see closer who is living in this caged manufacturing plant. These aren't uniforms of the SS we are wearing. There was once a Davidic star on my shirt. Though the star isn't there for the moment, it is still my identity. I am Jewish. I am a target of Hitler. Don't let me be a target of the British too. Will someone tell General Eisenhower this, please?

Yours, Anne M. Frank

Monday, August 14, 1944

Good morning Dearest Kitty,

There is a cold chill in the air, and we are still in August. A cold front, you ask? No. We have just been told that Tuesday is coming. When we first got here as new arrivals, we had no idea what Tuesday meant. Now that we are getting acclimated and being accepted into the population, the full truth is coming out. You see, Monday is selection day. Westerbork is not a retirement camp, it is a transit camp. We are told that every Monday, the Kampleiding chooses who will be transported out of Westerbork the following day. Most fear it is to Poland, to a place called Auschwitz, where rumors say the real nightmare begins and ends.

I had felt a peace at first knowing that much of the camp governance was handled by the Kampleiding, which was the leadership committee of German speaking Jews. Now, as we have learned more, I am afraid of this group and of their betrayal of our own people. These are Jews who, as I understand it, select other Jews to be shipped out to much harsher camps where death is often the verdict the minute a person boards the train. This must have been what Moses felt like when Korah tried to turn the people against him and Aaron, or what Jesus felt when his own disciple Judas betrayed him. How can these betray so easily? Do they not fear God?

Peter and I discussed this too. We are both afraid. I asked him the same question, "Do they not fear God?" It made me turn to Peter and ask him, "Peter, you have denied God, disliked God, and even taken His Name in vain. Do you see what people who deny Him do?" I think Peter was convicted a little, but not convinced.

Enough of that. We are in the punishment barracks. Who better to ship out than us? Oh, how I pray we won't be selected. We want to be free. We don't necessarily like it here, but we would rather be here than on one of those cattle cars. Pim and Mother led our prayers. Soon, we will see. They are calling us to formation.

Yours, Anne M. Frank

Tuesday, August 15, 1944

Dearest Kitty,

The selection was made yesterday. As I am writing to you in my mind, I am glad to report we are still here. I am hoping the war will be over soon. I don't know how many more Mondays I can take, nor do I know how many more Mondays I will have. It seems Tuesday is always around the bend. We may one day soon board the cattle cars – perhaps separately, maybe together. I will stop there. I can still not come to grips with the worse-case scenario, nor will I try.

Yours, Anne

Wednesday, August 16, 1944

Dearest Kitty,

Back to the battery brigade. We had a few sirens for the bombs dropping. Work stopped. The dust settled. The order was given. Back to the battery disassembly. How I wish the Nazi reign could be disassembled so easily. I am missing Miep. Every day, I would greet her with "Hello Miep, what's the news today?" I would love to know the answer to that. We all would. Propaganda is all we hear. They tell us that we are here to help the war effort, to bring victory. If we work hard, the Germans will win, and we can all go back to our homes. I would love to believe that, but I don't think the Fuhrer plans on any of us going back home when the war is over, especially if he wins. My back hurts as do my finger nails. What I wouldn't give to see that camp hairdresser about a manicure, but then again, she doesn't make rounds to the punishment side of town. I have developed a bad cough, but so has everyone. No sick day for those who cough. We all cough. Sometimes in boredom, we try to cough on cue and in rhythm. We try to make a song by timing our coughs and pitch just right. We smile and keep deconstructing the charge in front of us.

Mother is the best worker in our line. She works fast, is thorough, and is constantly being pointed to by our foreman as the one to emulate. She even helps us with ours so that we don't come under discipline. I

thought she loved Margot more than me, but she sure gives us equal help
and impartial care.

Yours, Anne Frank

Friday, August 18, 1944

Dearest Kitty,

There is nothing to report from the job. But, yesterday and today, the
eight of us have met and we continue to debate who might have betrayed
us. Pim says he is not as mad at the arresting officers as he is at the one
who sold us out. What harm were we doing anyone? We could understand Bep or Miep or even Mr. Kugler turning us in. They were doing
without. They were living in high risk. They would be rewarded for turning us in and their burden would be reduced exponentially. So naturally,
they were our first candidates to be tried in our jury of eight.

We went over each one. We had feared that Miep was beginning to
despise us as Jews. Antisemitism was rising all over Holland. She had
seemed irritated with us, and had even used a phrase "you people" when
the Van Daans were on a complaining rant. She quickly backtracked, but
the topic was on the table. Our fears had been growing in our secret Annexe, but Father did what he always does. He courageously addressed
the situation and met one on one with Miep. What a great visit he had.
All of our fears and suspicions were just due to Annexe fever making us
think the whole world was against us. It was not that way at all. Miep
was great after the visit, and I think she worked extra hard to alleviate
our fears.

Pim shared with us how ever since that time, Miep doubled her ef-
forts to care for us, often eating even less than we did, just so we could
have more. He saw her face when we were arrested. He had worked with

her a long time. That was not the face of guilt, but of extreme fear and sorrow. The debate was tabled for the time being. I am sure we will take up this topic again soon Kitty. If they don't, you and I will.

Yours, Anne Frank

Sunday, August 20, 1944

Dearest Kitty,

I know you are wondering why I am not talking about my love, Peter. To be honest, things are different between Peter and me now that we are out of exile. I am not sure how to explain it. He definitely is around a lot more girls. It was easier for him to like me when there were just two girls in his fish bowl. Margot was great for him and so was I. The difference was, I was more approachable. Margot wasn't. I am one to be proactive. Margot is more willing to let life and boys come to her. In Peter's lack of confidence and drive, wanting everything to be easy, I was the destined winner of his affection.

Now, there are more girls to be near and talk to. And, for me, there are more young men to visit with. It seems I have caught the eye of a few. This reminds me so much of when I was in school. I had many suitors but few suitable. There was my close friend, Hello, who loved me. You remember him? I saw Hello as a good friend, but nothing more. Then, there was the boy of my dreams, Peter Schiff – literally and figuratively. I may never know if I was his, but I know he was mine. And lately, Peter Van Daan. He is so different from the original Peter, but in my heart, I laid the dream Peter onto this Annexe Peter and saw in him what I wanted, perhaps more than what was there. I am starting to see that now.

I thought Peter Van D wanted my help; needed me to help him through life. I was bothered that he would lean on me when I wanted a man I could lean on like Pim. Now, I see Peter is standing on his own. Other girls are talking to him. He seems more confident and I wonder if he knows he owes that to me. Kit, I am confused. If I was still in upstairs confinement, I might take it harder, but if I was in upstairs confinement, this would not be happening. I have a hope now. Every day I see the blue sky. I see nature. I am living a life that is as close to normal as a Jewish person in German-occupied Holland can feel. Maybe it will work with him. Maybe it won't. But I do know this. We are friends. We have shared intimate secrets, descriptive conversations, our first kiss, and many nights looking out the window at the moon and stars in a shared embrace. No one can take that away. It may have been a stepping stone to maturity. I know I have grown, even more than the marks that Father made on the wall. If it is to be Peter, good. If not Peter, then someone better, I am sure. When I touch on the subject, Pim tells me to be patient. He was patient in finding Mother. Mother won in that deal. I hope I win the same way.

Yours, Anne M. Frank

Monday, August 21, 1944

Dearest Kitty,

I am sure you are wondering what we do each day. I haven't had time to let you know that have I? Well, today is Monday, so what we do on Monday is simple. We worry. Selection will occur today and transport will be tomorrow. It is our second since we have been made aware of what happens on this day. I dreamed last night that I was selected. My family was not. I cannot tell you what happened next in my dream.

Let me change the subject. What do we do each day? We are awakened each morning by a loudspeaker. We awake, get a little water and some bread, and then we head to the battery disassembly plant. There, we put on overalls because the work is so dusty with film getting all over us. We work all day, but not too fast. This way everyone can keep up, and no one gets in trouble. We work the full day, non-stop. Then at the end of the day, depending on when our guards say, the workday is over, we have time to meet with family and friends. It's a prison, but there is some form of humanity here. For this, we are eternally grateful.

Yours, Anne M. Frank

Tuesday, August 22, 1944

Dearest Kitty,

I had not shared with you before what I saw last Tuesday because I could not get over the fact that what I saw could easily have happened to me. They read out the names for the transport to Auschwitz. It was horrifying. Under threat of gunfire and promises of a better situation, men, women, and children were loaded into cattle cars. Some believed what they were being told and got in the car gladly. Others had to be pried away from their mother or father, begging to not be separated from them. There was no mercy and no chance for leniency. The list was the list. I can still hear some crying and screaming through the locked train car. Those whose loved ones were carted off just stood on the tracks inside the camp staring as the train pulled away. They would not look down or turn back. They watched as the train vanished out of sight, and they still stood for, what seemed like, hours on end, as if the train would change course and return.

I remember what Father told me about his Uncle Obed who raised cattle. He said every time they would take a calf to market, the momma cow would roam all over the pasture bellowing and looking for her baby calf. It would be sad to see that, but this is so much worse. The rest of us tried to comfort these who did lose family, but they were inconsolable. We have found the best thing to do is pray for them and give them time. What was worse, we knew that without some miracle, that would be our family one day – perhaps even in seven days. I can't bear the thought. My body begins to tremble as I let this roll around in my mind. I determine not to let it be there, but it is just as much there as the barbed fence when we leave our barracks. These fears sting me much like I believe that fence would if I dared touch it. I pray we never get transported out, and that the war will end even this very day.

Yours, Anne M. Frank

Wednesday, August 23, 1944

Dearest Kitty,

It is a new day, but we are still in the same place, doing the same thing. We get up. We are given something to eat that clearly lacks nutrition. We work perhaps twelve hours, if everyone behaves. They sometimes throw us some bread and water at lunch. Late in the day, they escort us back to our barracks for a light dose of whatever they can conceivably whip up. We have time together, and then we quietly go to our bunks for the night. In the barracks, none of us hardly speak. We are figuratively chained together; yet, no one makes any effort to get to know each other for fear that any relationship formed will soon be broken. It makes us not want to get close to anyone. Isn't the hurt of losing the family and friends we do have enough?

Back to the food for a minute. I get the idea that many people here were living in their nice apartments or even in forced areas of our city; yet, they did have food. They could have home cooking. They could go out. They took their ration cards, went to the grocery stores where Jews were allowed in the hours that were allotted. There were shortages but they managed. The next thing they know, they are here in Westerbork eating slim rations, poorly cooked and barely edible. Our inmate friends, besides the separation and transports, complain most about the food. It is in their gripes that I think about what we have endured for over two years. Bad food? We have eaten it. Isolated? We have felt that. Food shortages? We have had them. Separated from the world? We have experienced it.

It seems to me, Kitty, that we have prepared for this over two years. Though we hated going through that, it does seem that God has steeled us for days like these. In fact, in many ways, this is much easier than when we were in the Annexe hiding. At least we can make noise. We have nothing to hide. We have people to talk to other than the island of eight. And I can be outside some. I can see the sky, feel the breeze, and see the birds that I hear singing. I believe that no matter what we face, there are some good things; some gifts God has given to us. I feel on days like this that He is protecting us, even loving us. It's not just because I feel we are the chosen people, but because we are part of His Creation.

Yours, Anne M. Frank

Thursday, August 24, 1944

Dearest Kit,

After work today, Father, Mr. Van Daan, Dussel, and Peter joined us in the barracks yard. Yard usually denotes grass and landscaping, but clearly the grounds crew here felt dirt was easier to water. So, on this dusty ground, we all met. Peter brought up the usual conversation. Who turned us in? Father says we may have just been too careless in what we were doing and may have been seen in the process. Dussel, still as defensive as ever, said no. He really feels it may have been tied to the burglaries. Of course, he simply cannot fathom it would be because he was mailing letters to people exposing our nest. Nor can he attribute it to his own forays down to the Kugler office to work in the late hours of the night, with lights on and radio blaring. Oh no, it could not have been Dussel's fault!

He does have a point with regard to the burglaries, though I hate to agree with that man. When we look at the number of break-ins and note how each time they came closer and closer to our hideaway, even fiddling with the bookcase; it would seem they had an idea. When things are secret or kept out of reach, human nature says there must be something of value there. Perhaps the burglars were tired of the little booty of briefcases and radios, and were hoping for a bigger score.

The problem with these suspects is why would a burglar turn us in, just to expose themselves to the question, "What were you doing there at that time of night?" And, how many real criminals (I use the word "real" because we are labeled criminals for doing nothing but fighting to survive) run to the police. Their very vocation requires them to run from the police. I cannot understand why knowing "who" is so important to us. Would it make our stay here easier? If we knew for sure who did it, what damage could we do them? Pim says this, but he seems more intrigued by the question than the rest of us combined. When I write my book about the secret Annexe, Detective Anne will have to snoop this out. My readers, if I ever have any, will want some answers.

Yours, Anne M. Frank

Friday, August 25, 1944

My darling Kitty,

Fridays have a special feel to them. Before all this time in hiding, Friday was the day we looked forward to. It was a day for family. Even in the attic, we chose this day to often play games, role play, and entertain each other. I considered the eight of us in hiding as a family. To a degree, I would like our barrack mates to have that feeling also. So many are lonely, hurting, and afraid. We have known this feeling for over two years now. It is nothing new for us. We knew that at any point we could be arrested, but we chose to make the most of each day. Margot, who loves studying religion, reminds us constantly what the Bible says, "Make the most of the day while it is today." Now, as you know, Margot is very thoughtful, but passive. She is just as humble as she has always been and more willing to let life come to her. She says to make the most of the day, but it seems I have to be the one to do the making.

With that in mind, tonight before we went to bed, I started talking to the ladies on both sides of our wooden slanted hay holders they call beds. I asked them each to tell me what they thought was their best memory before the Nazis came to town. Jette spoke up. She is an older Jewish woman whose husband disappeared one day when he was going to the store with a ration card he had purchased from the black market. Jette waited and waited but he never showed up. She felt maybe it was past curfew and he decided to lay low until he was free to move again, but that wasn't the case. As best she can guess, he was picked up and questioned at the store over his ration card, and then carted away never to be seen again. Jette says her best memory was the first week after her marriage to Josef when they had settled in their first apartment. She said it was like a fantasy come true, a dream so hazy she fears it will evaporate. They didn't have much money, but they had some furniture and a few changes of clothes. In the evening, they would sit on their well-used, second hand divan after dinner. With no radio or distractions, they would share what they loved about each other and cast ideas of what the future held in store for them. It was all in front of them then. He would gently hold her in his arms, speak in a low, caring voice, confiding every hope and every dream he had. He wanted to make sure she never regretted her decision to be his wife. I tell you, Kitty, there wasn't a dry eye in the house.

All of a sudden, we weren't cloned workers in uniforms imprisoned against our will to the monotony of some master. We were people again. Izabel, a girl in her early twenties, on the other side of Margot and Mother, quietly raised her hand. No one gave her permission to speak because no one was in charge. We all just looked over at her which to her was permission enough. Izabel said her favorite memory was walking home from school, getting near her home, and smelling the supper emanating from her mother's kitchen window. The stronger the smell, the faster she walked. She said her mom made everything from scratch and was a perfectionist in what she produced. We could almost smell the food ourselves. Valentina who sleeps across from me, laughed and said "Cut it out, my stomach is growling, and my mouth is watering. You have taken this torture we're in to a higher degree!" We all laughed.

I was surprised, but Margot spoke. That's a mouthful right there. Margot spoke? In public no less? Without being asked? I piped up, "Oh ladies, watch for an eclipse! This is a rare occurrence!." Margot gave me the "Be quiet or I'll brain you" big sister look. I smiled and went quiet. Margot began to talk about Father. No, not just Father. Father and Mother. And me! She said her favorite memory was when we just moved to our apartment in Amsterdam. Father was starting his business. Mother was doing all she could to support him, along with the household. Margot, being older, told us how she remembered Father coming home late in the evening and how Mother made us all wait to eat until he arrived. We thought we would starve to death. Boy, that's a laugh here in this place. She said Mother would see through the window, Pim walking toward the house. She would tell us, "Father is home." We would then light out after him. Margot went first because she was faster than me, but I would be right on her heels. Margot would leap into his arms, and I would grab his leg. He would come walking into our home struggling to hang on to his office work, his briefcase, his oldest daughter, and his anchor called Anne on his leg. She said Mother would kiss him, hug us all, and then bring the greatest, sweetest words to our ears, "Let's eat!" Margot said that, plus the fact that every night Father and Mother came to tuck us in and say our prayers with us, were her greatest memories.

One by one Kitty, so many shared. Ursula, Renee, and even Elly told their stories. We really didn't even know these ladies' names much less their stories. It was late. We all had to go to work the next day. There are very few off-days in the Punishment Barracks. Things quietened down Kitty, and Mother kissed us both goodnight. Then she spoke softly in my ear, "Anne, I know I don't tell you this enough, but I love you and I am so proud of who you are." What a night! Mother was changing. Finally, I was feeling that she could indeed one day be seen as my mother.

Yours Darling, Anne

Sunday, August 27, 1944

Dearest Kitty,

Did you think we rode our chariot out of here since I gave you a day off? I have to tell you, since Friday night, things in the camp are looking so much better. It seems we are becoming the family that I had talked about. Last night there was more sharing. We worked Saturday and to-day with so much more harmony. It seems everyone is wanting to help everyone else. We have a comradery that we never imagined possible in this situation. We work hard, though we cough more, it seems, each day. We are discouraged that the work never stops, and our progress seems to never be realized. Each day, there are more batteries. Even in all this, work is easier when working with others. Misery loves company, and we are opening our eyes to the company we share.

I will have to say though that we are afraid of the coming selection. I wish I could be like you. I wish I could just receive letters telling me what is going on, feel for the person writing, and even pray for them in the safe confines of my normal life. I say that, but, Kitty, you are so dear to me. I would rather go through this than have you or anyone that I love face what we face. Besides, with you there and me here, it is easier for me to confide to you what we face. Jette has told us some things about the members of the Jewish committee that decides our fate each week. There is an effort to catch their eye during the week, to win their favor. We have shared this with Father and Mr. Van Daan. It seems they have heard the same thing. If only we can stay in good favor with these, perhaps we can avoid the transports until the end of the war. We have no money to give them for favor, but hopefully our work and our attitudes will be enough to stave off the worst. Westerbork is bad but not as bad as what it could be, and to a degree, not even as bad as the Annexe was.

Yours, Anne M. Frank

Monday, August 28, 1944

My dearest Kitty,

There was good news going around this morning on the day of the week, where morale is at its lowest. We were hearing that there may not be any more transports from here. Rumor had it that the war was nearly won. The Russians have made great inroads, as have the British and Americans. There was also talk that the shelling on the railroad tracks made the passage to Poland and other places impassible. How wonderful that would have been!

Our hearts sank when they had us line up in fives for a roll call. They read out the names of those selected to leave the camp. We are just sick. With each name read, I feared the next name would be Otto Frank or Anne Frank. By God's Grace, no Frank, Van Daan, or Dussel was called. Do you think the war will ever end? Dare I place any hope that we can sit out the rest of the war here?

Yours, Hopeful Anne Frank

Tuesday, August 29, 1944

Dearest Kitty,

This morning at roll call they gathered the people who were slated to leave. The guards gave extra rations to the people called this time and extra water. They have announced that this group of people are going to a better camp to work at an assembly plant. They were each given a pair of gloves to hold on to. It seemed to us that this was true, as the ones we saw go forward were bigger and stronger people, mostly men.

There were the usual tears and sad goodbyes. There were still those who stood on the railroad tracks looking out at the horizon as the train slowly set below it. It is pacifying to think that maybe these were being sent to work, as opposed to their deaths. We are told that the Germans often use this as a ruse to gather the people in a less resistant manner. We may never know where they went or if they will live. I just hope we don't have to go, and that we are never separated.

Yours, Anne M. Frank

Friday, September 1, 1944

Dearest Kitty,

Nothing to report this week but routine. Not only is the work continuing routinely, but the mood in our barracks has returned to isolation in the masses. We all had hoped for the end of transports. Our prayers of riding out the war together as a unit here versus a cattle car seem to have gone unanswered. It makes me wonder about God. We are called His chosen people, but we suffer worse than any other people. We revere His Name, though sometimes not as devoutly as He may like us to. Why are we singled out of all the peoples of the earth? We who are the least in number, why are they so quick to bring about our extinction? It was this way in the days of Esther. Hard labor, restriction, and enslavement was the lot of our people in the days of Moses. Moses? Where is our Moses? Where is our Esther who will stand on our behalf? Who will lead us out of this? Will General Eisenhower? Will Prime Minister Churchill?

Does any of this make sense to you? I feel bad even saying this to you, because the minute I say it, I am convicted. Hasn't God kept us together? Hasn't He fed and clothed us and kept us from harm? He fed Elijah in the wilderness, and He is feeding us too. Margot says that we, the clay, are not to shake our fist at the potter. I tell you, she reminds me more of Father each day. If Pim had a wig and was a little more graceful, I would swear he's sleeping next to me in my barrack. I want to change. I am changing, but I want to change more. I want to be more like Father and more like Margot. We pray each night for help, for protection, for provision, and I throw in silently a prayer for me to change. I am still fifteen, but I feel twenty-eight. I have come a long way, but it seems I have so much farther to go. Has any teen ever seen what I have seen, or been through what I have been through?

Yours, Anne M. Frank

Monday, September 4, 1944

Kitty,

Everything to report today. Nothing is routine. This captivity just took a nightmarish turn. I am in a cattle car. The door is bolted. We have seen the sun set and the sun rise, and still we're being rocked back and forth and ever forward. Mother, Father, Margot, and our annexed family are all here. There is a bucket in the middle of at least 70 of us for water and another bucket in the back corner for the bog or toilet. The thing is running over and being sloshed on whoever is standing near it. The whole car smells like the inside of a dank, stale, unflushed toilet. I had seen days like this when we were in hiding, but the smell is much worse even than the Easter weekend where break-ins were many and answers were few. I know Kitty. I am getting to that.

It was Sunday when we were rousted out of our barracks early. Roll call sounded. We rushed to our places. We were caught by surprise – the reading of the names. There on the tracks, sat an unscheduled train with at least 14 or 15 cattle cars attached. We had no idea what was going on.

This wasn't the much-feared Tuesday roll. That we could expect. We spent all week getting our minds right, and our emotions prepared for Tuesday. We had felt all other days were safe. Not so. We listened. Near the middle of the list, I was shocked to hear "Anne." That caught my attention. I started praying, please don't let it end with my last name. For just the fraction of a second, I felt guilty. It was as if I was fine if the name was "Anne Goldstein" or "Anne Sibley." I was convicted in that I was good if it were some other girl, or some other family having their loved one snatched away. I could not reason through the thought before the last name "Frank" was spoken. Mother gasped. Margot wrapped her arms around me. They would have no time to comfort me, because the next name was "Edith." "Edith Frank." Then "Margot Frank" followed by "Otto Frank." As we made our way forward to the SS guard who was directing us hurriedly and forcefully to an awaiting cattle car with mouth wide open ready to engulf us, we heard behind us the names of Albert Dussel, along with the Van Daans, including Peter.

I don't know what car the others are in, but the Franks are together. Pim has placed himself between us and the rest of the sardines in this little tin box. We take turns sitting because there is no room. We learn how to sleep standing, only because we can lean against each other, and we are squeezed so tight that no one is able to fall to the floor. The smell is worse than any rotten fish. I have been able to press my face against a small round hole in the metal of the car. I don't know if it is a bullet hole or a missing screw, which could easily be why this thing rattles. It's not much relief, but it is some. I have offered to share that little hole with Margot and Mother. We can hardly speak to Pim. There is much wailing and weeping. It is dark in here and the stench is unbearable. I never have thought of Hell much. I know there is eternal life and eternal death. I have caught glimpses of eternal life and God's Presence looking at the sky on a spring day, studying the blooms on the trees and the brilliant greenery abounding everywhere. I don't know if I can say it, but it seems

that on days like those, I have felt God's gentle Hand rest on my shoulder. Today, I can say I have now caught a glimpse of eternal death where
darkness, pain, and stench is all there is. Masses are crowded together in
fear and torment, and God seems nowhere to be found. I wonder if Peter
feels this. I wonder if he is rethinking his theology now.

Where are we going? Father thinks Auschwitz. Mother says she is
praying for a factory in Germany. It's too long a ride to be Holland. And
Margot thinks we have traveled too far to still be in Germany. That
would mean Poland. Kitty will you pray for us? It seems we could be
going to Heaven soon or to Hell even sooner. At this moment, we have
no idea. Hades seems to be our state-of-being for the moment.

AUSCHWITZ-BIRKENAU

Oh Kitty,

All I can say is *unübersehbarer Schaden, schrecklich, entsetzlich, nie zu ersetzen*. That sounds more descriptive than what it means, "indescribable loss, terrible, awful, irreplaceable." We arrived at the concentration camp, Auschwitz. It was the most horrible feeling I have ever felt. I was sick to my stomach. They stopped inside this barbed enclosure of electrified fences on both sides, with a train track in the middle. Over the loudspeakers, we heard them shouting, "The door is about to open; leave everything in the car; come out and line up quickly." Of course, the first part of the instruction didn't apply to us. We haven't had anything since they arrested us in the Annexe.

The train door slid open and there were neatly dressed uniforms covering hateful looking men, holding whips, vicious dogs, and machine guns. All glared with guns pointed at us. The guards started shouting, repeating what the loudspeaker had said, "Leave everything in the train car, and we will get it to you later." They told us get out, no trouble, or they would mow us down on the spot. One guard said he wished we would bring some trouble. It would make things easier for them. We did what we were told. We have been doing that a lot lately, just out of reflex. People fought to keep their stuff, but more fought to hold on to their loved ones. We were no different. Mother and I held onto Father, while Margot held onto Mother. We were a huddled mass walking together as one man with eight legs. The guard shouted, "Men to the right, women and children to the left." That's not what we wanted. Father delayed, so a guard struck him on the side of his head. Father looked at us as if to say, "It will be alright," as he was shoved to his line, rubbing his head from the blow.

We, on each side of Mother, made our way to the line for women and children. We were formed in a line of fives. There were a lot of us, and it took a very long time, but methodically, with each group, a deciding officer pointed to each person in the group of fives. With another command, he yelled, "You and you go left. You three go right." As I watched this unfold, the older women, the sickly, and it seemed all the children were pointed to the left. Most of the children were separated from their mothers. Someone asked a soldier near us, "What will they do with the people on the left?" He gave a calm, reassuring answer, "They'll be alright. The kids have a school they will attend, and their moms can work during the day and be reunited with their children at night. The older ladies will have their own barracks to rest in and can do sewing and knitting for our camp. If they are sick, we will get them the care they need." That sounded so good and humane.

I never thought I could refer to a Nazi soldier with such a word, but that's what it sounded like. We were hardly fooled though. We knew these soldiers used every ounce of deceit to get their way, including telling people that a trainload of people was going to work in an assembly plant. We had no doubt that the horrible smoke and smell that crossed our lines was the destiny of that trainload, as well as everyone here. I overheard one of the guards say under his breath, "Yes, that's right. They will all be taken care of, as they ascend up our chimneys."

Mother, Margot, and my group were up. I prayed. Mother and Margot looked down, but I looked the officer right in the eye. The officer asked me a question, "How old are you?" I asked, "Sir?" In his broken accent, I wasn't sure what he had asked, or if he was talking to me directly. He demanded a little louder, which scared me, "How old are you?!" I told him, "Fifteen years old, Sir." He then said to me, Mother, and Margot, "You three to the right." To the two next to us, "You and you to the left." The two beside us seemed happy with the choice. I watched them as they made their way down the lit path beside the barbed wire. They were headed to where the chimneys were. And, they were hugging their children with joy, saying and believing, "It's going to be alright children." I never saw those people again. What about Pim? He had lost so much weight and he looked much older than his mid-fifties. What line was he pointed to? I feel I know, but I dare not feel.

The girls of our family joined, it seemed, several hundred more. In typical German efficiency, we were divided into three groups and sent to three different stations. Our group was led to a shower where we were forced to disrobe, all of us, in front of these soldiers. No man had ever seen me naked before. I once had the most intimate talks with Peter on such subjects. He was the only boy I had ever discussed things so private. I had made a commitment in my dating him or any boy that I would let them kiss me on the lips, but nothing more. As interested as I was in sex and the sexual differences between men and women, I saw my body as a wedding gift to be seen and unwrapped for the first time on my wedding day by my husband. This was not my wedding day. But, I was being unwrapped not just for one man, but for many men – none I knew and none I had ever seen before. I felt they would stare at me, but they seemed to just glaze over as hundreds of naked women, young and old stood in front of them. I assumed they were like doctors who, after examining so many undressed women daily, were no longer aroused at the sight. True or not, I held on to that thought. It was the only way I could bear it. We were sprayed by a stinging-type fluid that had a strong ammonia smell.

I had hoped now they would let us redress, but they did not. We were then paraded to a barber type set-up and forced to wait in line. We were tired, thirsty, and afraid. We were worried for those who were not with us and worried for those who were with us. We were weak and so drained. We moved forward as if in an assembly line driven by conveyor belts. I did not feel my legs move, but they did so on command. I did notice all these nude bodies around me. I had only seen maybe four naked women in my life – me, Mother, Margot, and a friend from school. With what snap I had, I was amazed at the variety of female bodies. Each were so different. Some sagged. Some seemed flat. Some had parts that fell out of place. Some were heavy and some were thin. Some were old and wrinkly. Others looked as if puberty had never come.

Wobbling forward, Mother stepped up in front of us. With no tenderness, they sheared Mother's hair down to her scalp in reckless haste. She had always taken care of her hair with a special pride. Truly, her hair was the most beautiful of all of us. I condemned her a lot throughout our lives for many deserved critiques, but her hair never once made the list. I loved her hair and hoped I would enjoy the same fullness when I grew older. I could tell that she was greatly saddened as they buzzed her hair and let it drop right in front of her eyes. They were rough, pushing her head this way with one buzz, that way with the next. It didn't take a full minute, and she had no hair at all. She was about to cry until she looked up at us with our tears rolling down our cheeks. It was then she forced a smile. She mouthed, "It's alright. It didn't hurt at all." Then it was Margot's turn. She wept the whole time through. I heard her ask the soldier, "Why?" He gave no response except to say "Next!", looking at me. I climbed up in the wooden chair, and no sooner did I get my full weight down, he had already lopped off two paths. Mine was gone quicker than Mother's but took a little longer than Margot's. I took the haircut much harder than Mother or Margot. I had loved my hair, cared for my hair, and received praise for my hair in school. I loved to take my fingers and twirl my hair with them. I think it made the boys see me all the cuter for it. Now it is gone. I didn't cry, but I sure wanted to. I wanted to look in a mirror, but judging by my loved ones' heads, I knew I had seen more than I needed to. If I had caught a glimpse of myself at that moment, I would have fallen apart in front of them all, a shameful sight over something so unimportant when compared to staying alive.

I hoped now we could get some clothes on. It was September, but it was deep into the night, and I was cold from the wet disinfectant and from the nervous sweat brought on by fear. The cold air hit my naked body, and I was starting to feel sick. Back when we were free, I can remember feeling fine one minute and then being hit by this sickness or fever the next. It's like walking into a tree branch unexpectedly. That's the sick I was feeling in the cool night air. No clothes were offered. There was another line to get into. I saw women walking away rubbing their arm. I thought they had received some kind of shot, but then the more slowly they passed to the next station, the better view I was able to catch. They were being tattooed. Each and every one of them, and every one of us. Like cattle to the brand, and slaves departing the ship, we were about to receive our mark.

I stood in front of a young, nice looking soldier. Had he not been in a Nazi uniform, he could have gone to my school. He looked the age of Peter Van Daan, and in some ways resembled him. When I caught his eye, he looked me in the eye, and then he looked up and down my naked body. I wanted to pull behind something, cover up, but I had nothing to pull in front of me. I lifted my arms to cover my breasts hoping the table would cover my lower part. I was feeling more exposed at that moment than throughout the rest of the night's ordeal. He asked my name as he went from my eyes, to my breasts, to my hips, rising from his chair to look at my legs, and then back again. He smiled as if this was funny. He said again, "Your name?" I told him, "Anne Frank." He wrote it down to the right of a blank column on his spreadsheet. I didn't want to say my name. It's one thing to be seen naked, but another thing for them to know my name while I stood naked before them. He then told me to hold out my arm. I didn't want to because that would uncover my breast. He didn't ask nicely the second time, so I put it out there, and he no longer looked at my body. He took his instrument and sloppily and painfully marked me "A-25237." He then wrote to the left of my name, in that column reserved for a number that followed many other numbers above it, "A-25237." He then told me that this was to be my number for the rest of my time here. He said, "You are A-25237. When you hear that number, that's you. You better respond. It will be your number called for work detail, your number series called for meals, your number if you are to be disciplined, and your number if you are to be transported. It will be your number at roll call each morning and your number at roll call each evening. Be sure you respond to it or you will not make it out of here alive. Just a friendly warning."

With that I was dismissed. I walked naked from that auction stand slowly as to give Mother and Margot time to catch up with me. We were led to a barrack, naked, disinfected, shaved, and tattooed in front of the men. I was surprised to see a level of respect that I never dreamed existed for women. Instead of staring at us, the prisoners in our party, all turned their heads to look the other way. They felt for us. They wished to not add to our humiliation. I will always remember that.

It was only inside this long cold barrack that we had striped clothes waiting just inside the entrance. There were no sizes, so we grabbed a ragged dress and negotiated with our neighbors to find the best fit. They were old and torn, mended and patched. I wondered who had worn these before me. Was the smoke I was smelling the person who once wore these slave clothes?

In grave fear, a woman asked the guard, "What will happen to us now?" He said, "You will work! *Arbeit Macht Frei.*" They were telling us that work will make us free. Was this a promise or a pacifier for what was to come? They marched us to our barracks. What grieved me most was that with each step, I was farther away from Father. I could not bear the distance, nor the fear for him and us. Then they led our group to Barrack 29. This was to be where we would stay. Behind this foyer, for lack of a better term, were three rows of wooden bunks – two against the walls (one on each outer wall), and one in the middle with two sides. There were already many women there. At first glance, the barrack seemed full, but as it turned out, room had just been made for us as some of the recent residents had been "relocated" a few hours before. Relocated where? I had my fears. We were forced into wooden, slat covered bunks. There was a foul odor. The mattress, if you can call it that, was perhaps one-half an inch thick and when the eight of us crowded into a place that could not sleep two, fleas jumped up and began to rest on us. I had seen fleas up in the attic on Peter's cat and many more at Westerbork, but they were nothing as wretched as these. I know Dussel (if he is alive) is not happy about this one bit. So, this is Auschwitz. All I can say is *unübersehbarer Schaden, schrecklich, entsetzlich, nie zu ersetzen* – indescribable loss, terrible, awful, irreplaceable. I was crowded next to Margot who was pushed against Mother. In between bits of slumber, I cried all night long.

I hope still Yours, A-25237

Thursday, September 7, 1944

Dearest Kitty

What day is it? Oh, that's right, Thursday, September 7th. Thank you for reminding me. I am in a horrific, perhaps self-imposed daze. I speak to you because you help me. I also note the day to you so that I can know what day it is. Each day matters and each day is a marker. I hope it marks the days I am living and not a countdown for the time that I have left.

We were awakened this morning with a harsh sound. We got out of our crowded, flea-infested beds, and were told to make ready for roll call. All we have on are some clogs we were given when we got here and a dress of some sort, nothing else. We have no clothes underneath. Of all the indignities we have endured, I didn't tell you this one yesterday, because I tried not to think of it. My head was not all they shaved. They shaved every hair on us. I say "they" shaved us. It would be one thing if they would have let us shave ourselves in the private areas; but no, they shaved us there too, and they did so very roughly.

I have met a lady named Ronnie. She seems to be handling this a little better than us. There was a pan of dark water for us to drink from. Some called it coffee, and some called it something else. I know it was definitely something else. There are few cups so we group up around a particular cup. We were told this would be all we would get, so drink sparingly. Ronnie took the cup, dipped it into the pan, and then told us, "Let's each take three sips each. If there is anything left, we can then pass it around and take one sip each until it is gone." This seemed like a great idea. She took three sips, we counted. She then handed it to me. I took three sips, and they all counted. It was terrible, but it was liquid. I passed it to Mother who passed it to Margot first, and then Margot gave it to Mother after her three sips. It made its way around a couple of times. They gave us a piece of bread, and then directed us to the latrine.

What a nasty and unsanitary place this is. I had thought our Annexe toilet was not very clean. I had thought relieving ourselves in the waste basket while under duress in the upper room of Father's business was as bad as it could get. I was wrong. The smell of urine and feces was overpowering. There were three rows of what looked like cement troughs for livestock, with a hole every so many centimeters. It was in these holes we were to do our business. Smears of dung and yellowing puddles sat on the opening of each toilet hole. I had to relieve myself, but here? How? Am I to sit on that and get whatever is on there on me? There was no toilet paper to wipe it down. No spices to tame the smell. Some women climbed up on top and squatted to urinate. Others, in a fog, just plopped down on top, did their business and left. What was I to do? I looked at Margot. She had no idea. I looked at Mother and she said, "Let's try this." She went first. She backed up against it, lowered herself, tightened her stomach muscle, strained her thighs and was able to accomplish the necessity without ever touching the base. We did the same. It was hard, but possible.

We were then called out for roll call. They told us how things would go the first day, and then said it would not be retaught again. The next roll call, if things were not absolutely up to their standards, there would be Hell to pay. The man who said this, emphasized it by slapping his hand with his whip. The other guards looked and nodded approvingly. We formed rows of five, which we had done at Westerbork. They then told each row to hold their arms forward touching the shoulders of the person in front of us. We all did this, though my arms were shorter than Mothers, and hers shorter than the woman next to her. Whoever had the longest arms in the row set the distance for our row. They said this is how we are to do it each time roll call is summoned. This allows the SS guards to walk between us and inspect us. To get their point across, they singled out a woman in the row two ahead of us. They felt she wasn't as energetic about this exercise and they beat her to a pulp. I heard her screaming and pleading in a language that sounded Russian. They drug her away. I never saw her again, but we all got the point. One other thing, just as I was turning to say something to Margot, the guard looked at me and said, "There will be no talking in rank!" I looked forward, chin in, head up.

Roll call followed for what seemed like days. It did last for hours. We all had to get used to our number, so that when our number was called, we could respond. I thought that if anyone escaped, this would be a good way to cover for others, but escape how? Escape where? Just as the trains were bolted shut, so was this camp. I wondered if the only people escaping this place were being seen floating over our rank and file in billows of smoke.

Once roll call was over, we were assigned our task. Mother, Margot, and I walked together as if we were three people bound by a tether. Our job was to move big rocks from one end of the camp, where they lay, to the other end. I looked at the carts on the railroad track and thought we would load them in the cart, and then they would be carried to the other end where hopefully some other lucky souls could unload them. I was wrong. Carts are for German soldiers. So then, how did we move those rocks, you ask? We had to carry them. Pick them up and walk them to the other side. It would make sense that the bigger and stronger women would take the bigger and heavier stones, but human nature says that each woman is on her own and should pick up the smallest and lightest available. I found something redeeming here at that moment, Kitty. The strong women willingly carried the heavier stones. Younger, smaller women like me and Margot were given the smaller, lighter ones. I don't know how long this kindness will last, but like having a man open the door for you, it is a courtesy of which you take advantage.

Saturday, September 9, 1944

We are back in our bunks after a hard day of endless labor. My arms, legs, and back are killing me. I have always had back pains. I think it is because of my rapid growth those last few months in the Annexe. We still have a lot of rocks to move. A truck came this morning and brought more for us. I have no idea what they will do with all these rocks. I suppose they will have the men or some laborers build something with them. They are quite heavy, and they are sure piling up on the other end of the camp. They better get started soon.

We had a light rain last night, and there were puddles waiting on us when we began our work. I had the chance, walking back for my next load, to look down at the puddle and see myself. I was appalled. The reflection looking back at me surely was not Anne. I, Anne Frank, a girl from Holland looked down and saw a boy looking back at me. I mentioned it to Margot. I asked her point-blank, "Is that me? Is that what I look like to you?" She said that I will always look like her beautiful, sweet baby sister. That didn't answer the question. I looked like a boy. I thought back to when we first moved into the secret Annexe. Peter and I were young and not in love for sure. We were trying to entertain our cast of characters in the Annexe, so Peter dressed as a girl and I dressed as a boy. That was fun then. Now, it's not so funny.

All day long, I caught myself reaching for the end of my hair to wrap it around my fingers. It wasn't there to twirl. I wondered when it would grow out again, and how long would it take? Judging by the other prisoners who have been here a while, that is something they won't let happen. I hate this place. I hate where we are. I hate what has happened to us. And I hate Father is not here.

Sunday, September 10, 1944

Dearest Kitty,

Work has been monotonous. We are still moving stones. Each day, I feel more soreness. They hardly feed us. We are all so very thirsty. We see warning signs on the water we get from the faucets. Some cup their hands and drink from puddles when they find one. Our fear constantly is the consideration of what made the puddles. We fear dysentery or diarrhea. This is bad but I dare not get sick. Mother reminds us daily, "Stay strong." When she isn't reminding us, I am reminding her. We each have our moments.

Let me break away from that for a moment. I lay here in this bed in a spoon type fashion. Wait a minute, Kitty, a lady's legs are feeling numb. We all have to roll at the same time. With a word, we roll. Now I am not as comfortable, but what can I do? I look at my face and appearance. With our haircut, we all look the same. I look at our clothes: tattered, frayed, and mended. We look the same dressed as we do naked, except naked there are sags and features that are more discernible. I look at my left arm, and staring back at me is the number A-25237. I ask myself and you, why are we made to look this way, and why are we marked by numbers and not names? I have been thinking about this as I carry the heavy boulders because that is what the rocks become by the end of the day. I wish I had my hair like Samson. Maybe then I could bear under these. Didn't the Philistines cut his hair to weaken him too? That could be the case.

The Nazi machine wants to weaken us and break us. I see that occurring. Yesterday, mid-afternoon, a woman started screaming that she could not take it anymore and she threw herself into the wire. With a great buzzing and a smell of smoke very similar to what comes from the chimneys at the end of the camp, she was dead. The guards cursed her and yelled at us to look at her laying there. "Let this be a warning to you. Don't touch the fence. And, if you do, we will let your body lay out and rot for all to see." I was sick at my stomach.

Oh Kit, where would I be if I did not have you to talk to. If only that woman had you. I think you are the one who keeps me sane. I dare not share some of the things with Mother or Margot. And, we are given such little time to visit here that even if I could tell them what I feel, when would we have time or energy to converse?

Gratefully Yours, Anne M. Frank

Monday, September 11, 1944

My dear Kitty,

More stone slave work today. We worked harder today because the barrack next to ours complained. In the middle of the night, we heard loud trucks pull up, orders were given, and the barracks were emptied. The women screamed, but rallied in obedience. This morning they were gone. Where? Smoke rises from the chimneys. We are being told by some older inmates here that there is a gas chamber waiting for the weak, the weary, the disobedient, and the irritable. We strive not to be any of these.

Back to our appearance discussion from last night. Why do they make us look alike? Why cut our hair; all our hair? We have to lift our skirts from time to time so they can see if we need shaving. It is horrifying. Thankfully, I haven't had my period since we left Westerbork. As I see others having theirs, blood running down their legs as they work, I pray I never have another, but I know my time is coming. Mother and Margot had theirs. For some of their bread, they were able to get a rag to wipe themselves and manage. That is a terrible trade-off, bread or blood.

I remember reading a book not too long before our forced evacuation from our loft. It told of a boy who loved to hunt, but he hated to clean what he had killed. He just could not bear to look at the face of his kill. He loved animals, and he loved hunting. He believed that you only kill what God has made for food because that is why God gave it. He had a dilemma. He soon found a solution that would enable him to deal with his love of hunt and food with his love of the animals and birds he pursued. If he cut the head off his gun's victim, he would then be cleaning a headless carcass. Once the head was gone, it no longer reminded him of a pretty, furry animal or a beautiful, winged bird. I wonder. I wonder if the reason the Germans shave our heads and give us numbers is so that what little reserved conscience they have left is soothed. They are treating human beings like animals, but if dressed a certain way with names removed, they are only dealing with objects and not people. I wonder.

Yours, Anne M. Frank

Tuesday, September 12, 1944

Dearest Kitty,

Forget about today. I don't want to talk about it. I just went through the motions all day covered in bereavement. I can't help thinking about Pim. We had a woman, who was supposed to have been going to the latrine, slip into our barrack because she had heard some of us were from Amsterdam. She asked if any of us had seen her daughter. They had been separated when we arrived, and she was frantic. Now that we are being made more aware of the gas chamber and the daily selections, her fear is that her daughter has been gassed. Her hope is that they are just separated by barracks and work detail. We were so sorry for her, especially when Mother gets to hold me and Margot each night. No one had any idea, but after she left, Freda, a lady bunking near us, said she saw her daughter go with the sick and the elderly in the line to the left.

I once said that I could handle Mother dying, but that I could not live without Father. I had vanquished this thought from my mind, but tonight, it has returned in startling realism. Pim was in his mid-fifties. He was thin and weaker than most men because he had sacrificed for us in the Annexe. He also carried the load of worry for us, his workers, and his company. He was separated from us when they divided the men from the women. The men were subdivided like we were, but we lost sight of them. Any time I see a man in stripes about Father's age, I look at the man with a hope it is Father. No sign of him yet. Mother says Father has to be alive. He is smarter and better with people. If he made it past the first selection (which she was sure he did), he has the skills to make it past the future selections. I just hold to a hope she is right.

Yours, Anne

Friday, September 15, 1944

My dearest Kitty,

We had hit a wall. All of us were just done. It is hard to imagine losing the will to live after just nine or ten days of being here. It came sooner than we thought. Being the youngest in this barrack and having the hardest time keeping up with the physical requirements, I am more silent here. The pluck that Margot admires has been plucked from me, I fear.

In our despair, the woman who shares my cup in the morning, Ronnie asked the ladies in our area to share their favorite memories before we lost our freedom. This was so refreshing and a little self-gratifying. I had done the same thing at Westerbork, but during much easier circumstances. No one was willing to share at first, but a woman in her late twenties introduced herself as Lena. She told of how she and her husband had met in school at Antwerp shortly before the Germans were flexing their muscles. The Jews in her town were being greatly restricted and they had a fear that they would soon lose the freedom to marry. They loved each other so much and decided together or apart, long life or short, they wanted to formalize their love with the covenant of marriage. She described how handsome her husband was. She told how funny he could be, but at the same time be the hardest worker of any she had ever seen. Her father even said so. Not long after they were married, he went out to get some milk and never returned. A neighbor said they saw a police officer pick him up. He was never seen again. She assumes he is at best in our predicament somewhere or at worst dead, which was more likely. Why was she sharing this story? She said because they did the most important thing when they could. They solidified their love in marriage. It was actually very beautiful.

Ronnie asked for someone else to share. Finally, she said, "Mrs. Frank, you have two beautiful daughters here with you. Please, what is the most treasured memory you have?" Mother looked at us and smiled. She said, "I have many beautiful memories of me and the girl's father, Otto. I cannot say one is more treasured than the other, but I will share my latest. I had a dream the other night that we were back in Amsterdam. The girls were young. Margot was just learning how to ride a bicycle and Anne was still in a stroller. Every evening when Otto got off early from work, he loved for us to take a walk together as a family before supper. I think this is why our youngest Anne loves being outside so much. Otto would walk beside Margot as she struggled riding her bike without tipping over. I pushed Anne behind in her stroller, fighting her every step of the way. She was constantly trying to climb out to catch up with Margot. She would often cry because she wanted to ride a bike like Margot. She could not understand that there is an order of things and steps to maturity. Margot was always out front and Anne was always reaching from behind. I truly have been blessed with a beautiful family, a great husband, and two beautiful and unique daughters!."

Wow! Mother is changing. We are told that God works everything for good to them who love Him. I am seeing this first hand. In this living tragedy, my Mother (I can't believe I call her "my") is blossoming into the woman and mother I always longed for in her. We held each other a little tighter as other women shared. Our barrack was becoming a family like the one we formed with the Westerbork ladies. The only difference was this place was much harder, and the ties that bound us together were being broken much more often and in much more unthinkable ways.

I wanted to share about you Kitty, but I felt the ladies would think of me in a different way. Plus, I didn't want to elude to the fact that I had letters written to you where we were hiding. I still cannot imagine what damage those may have done if they have been found.

Yours, Anne M. Frank

Saturday, September 16, 1944

Dearest Kitty,

Last night was good tonic. We all woke up with renewed strength and a feeling of support from every lady near us. I hope other women are finding this where they are. It is hard to live on an island. So often I would have felt alone, if not for you. Now I see a need for others too. You can't go to the yard with me. You aren't able to carry these stones. For that, I am glad. I never want anyone I love to do this. I already have my visible family here doing this.

I am also helped by the fact that I dreamt last night of Grandma. She stood before me, smiling in brilliant white. She told me that she loved me and that everything will be alright. I asked her how she knew that and she answered that she had been through such suffering too. Grandma said God is with me, and that there will be an end to this struggle and pain. She said when it is over, it will all have been worth it. I am not sure what all that means. I have no idea how any of this can be worth it? But, I did find a sense of peace, which I needed. It seemed Heaven touched earth last night in my dream, and earth touched Heaven in our time of sharing.

Yours, Anne M. Frank

P.S. I know I don't have to end my conversations or verbal letters to you with Anne M. Frank. So why do I do it, you ask? Because for one, I want to be remembered. And, two, I am not a number. I am a person, a human being whom they are doing this to. They may want to forget that, but I will not forget. I refuse to be just another unknown, inconsequential number in their meat grinder.

Monday, September 18, 1944

Dearest Kitty,

I want to answer a question that I am sure you have. What of Mrs. Van Daan? She is here. But, she has blended in with another group of ladies in our barrack. Her group is composed of women who before the war and capture were of the higher society sorts. That's fine with us. She is very kind to us, and we face none of the drama with her that we used to. Besides, here there is no room for animosity. I tease a bit about the personality make-up of our former Annexe family, but the reality is I love them and appreciate them more as time passes. I am so grateful that we had our time together. We learned many valuable lessons together. I feel it has made us stronger now that we are here.

Mummy Van Daan took time in our bunks last night. We had a good catch-up visit, and then our conversation went back to the familiar refrain of who turned us in. The more we suffer, the more we vilify and condemn the person or persons who are responsible for us being here. Westerbork was one thing, but Auschwitz? This is a place where blame just has to be laid.

We have all thought about it. My mind keeps going back to Mr. van Maaren. Bep had told us that after he had become warehouse manager subbing for the sick Mr. Voskuijl, he took on an air of pompous, superior authority. Where Father said Mr. Voskuijl was friendly but firm with the employees, Mr. van Maaren managed through intimidation. He questioned those under him, demanding they prove their innocence when they were under his suspicion. He criticized those above him, thinking he could run the enterprise better. It was van Maaren who wanted to have access to every nook and cranny of the building. This is why he was always curious about the Annexe and the attic. Mother said that Miep had shared with her how he had confronted Mr. Kugler on many occasions about the restricted place above their heads. Often Mr. Kugler would put him off by saying, "That part of the building belonged to the business next door."

Van Maaren also seemed to be around every corner, spying out when people left, when people returned, and questioning their timing and trips, per Mr. Kugler. This seemed odd and perhaps was just a sneaky man being sneaky. But with all the break-ins and thefts, it stood to reason that a burglar would want to know what people were doing and when they were doing it, so that any theft could be calculated. Kugler didn't think he was stealing, just nosy. In our Annexe women's group at Auschwitz, we disagreed with Kugler. We finally decided that van Maaren was a likely suspect, though Mrs. Van D wasn't fully convinced. Perhaps he saw a chance to take over the business and become the lead, if only he could get Kugler and Kleiman out of the way. He once asked Kleiman why they continued to follow Otto Frank's procedures when he had been gone for so long. The inference was, "unless Otto Frank was still around?" Mr. van Maaren could have easily deduced that Otto Frank may still be running the business unseen, perhaps in the upper part of the building, along with family and others. He had seen and heard plenty of evidence to believe he was not alone in the building at night and on weekends. I think he thought that if our friends got caught hiding us, van Maaren could get rid of us and those who stood in his way. The impedance for him was nothing more than a bookcase waiting to be removed.

Sleep on that, dearest Kitty. Detective Anne has given you a tasty morsel to help toward the solution of this long sought-after mystery. It really doesn't matter though, does it? We are here no matter who turned us in. We have no power to do a thing about it. I say it does matter because in our minds we can convict and carry out the verdict to a fate even worse than our own.

Yours, Anne M. Frank

Tuesday, September 19, 1944

Dearest Kitty,

It has been a dreadful day today. We had roll call early this morning. We were rustled out of bed by the Kapos before dawn. We rushed out of our beds as if there was a fire-drill. It reminded us of the worries we had in the Annexe as to what we would do in case of a fire in our building. We were rushing out the door, passing our normal ration of bread and watered down something which they call "coffee." It seems there was a rumor among the guards that one of our numbers had escaped somehow. We lined up, roll call sounded and sure enough, someone was missing. They love to torture us here by going slow in roll call, making us stand at attention for hours on end. At first thought, you would not think it hard to stand for numbers being called, but remember how many there are of us. I have no exact count, but the numbers called out go on without ceasing. Every hour or so, we assume we are near the end just to find there are hours more to go. We never get used to this. Sometimes, people faint in line from hunger or thirst or bone-weariness. They are already famished and strength-zapped, but the guards beat the dead horse any way. A year ago, this would have made me want to stand up and say something. I have always been known for my honest facial and verbal displays. But now the spirit is beaten down. I am not as concerned about the equality of women or into political commentary. My only concern (and I think I speak for most of us) is survival.

As I stood there, I began to think about my ambitions and how radically priorities change when harsh realities set in. I want to be known, still. I want to make a difference, to have the whole world take notice. I don't guess that part of my fabric will ever leave. As much as I want that, do you know what I want more than anything right at this moment? I want an evening meal with my Father, to wash before bedtime and brush my teeth. I want to put on my nightie and have Pim and Mother say my prayers with me, to be tucked in, and to sleep in an actual, flea-free bed. I had that for two years, and I complained. Before our time in the Annexe, I had a much wider fishbowl in which to swim, and I complained then too. When everything is stripped away, what is most important becomes glaringly clear, and what we once took for granted is now the greatest treasure.

To be famous would be great. To be free would be even greater. For the war to end would be wonderful. For me and my family to exit our part of the war would be far better still. I am forced, based on lessons learned, to look more at what I have right now. I have my health, though I have noticed a tiny rash on my stomach. I have Margot with me, and Mother too.

My thoughts were interrupted. The final number was read. We were released to go back to our barracks and get our morning piece of black bread, and share a bucket of cooling floating coffee grounds. With that, I went out to work beside Margot and Mother. It was just another day in a holding place somewhere between earth and Hell.

Yours, Anne M. Frank

Friday, September 22, 1944

Dearest Kitty,

Just for your ears, Kitty; Mother has not been eating. She keeps giving us her portion of bread and soup, saying she is full or she has eaten already. We know better. I am getting greatly concerned for her strength. I don't want to lose Margot or Mother in the next selection. I think Mother is thinking the same. She doesn't want to lose me or Margot.

The rock detail is so very hard. We finally got the rocks moved from one side of the property to the other and were ready for our next assignment, which we hoped would be easier. Now they tell us there has been a change in plans. They have decided to build whatever it is on the other side. So, we have to move the rocks back almost to the exact place they were before. The work is grueling and it makes no sense at all. It's as if they are just making stuff up for us to do, so they can drain every last ounce of life out of us before they kill us.

I am growing weaker, but Margot and Mother seem to be holding up pretty well, all things considered. I have no idea how much weight we have lost, but we didn't have that much to lose to begin with. I was slapped over the back today by a whip from one of our lady tyrants. She thought I was slacking. I just was scratching a persistent itch I am having. I am sure it is just the flea bites from our bunks, but it's driving me crazy. I am struggling to dictate to you right now because of it, and I am struggling to sleep. If I am not swatting away the fleas, I am scratching the itches and whelps.

Yours as I am scratching, Anne

Sunday, September 24, 1944

Good morning Miss Kitty,

I am back in my bunk earlier than normal this morning. We were rousted out of bed for a health check. We have to totally undress, run out to roll call formation, get our spacing right, and then in fives go before the doctors for a humiliating, but not thorough examination.

First, the male dentist checked our teeth. I immediately wondered if they had Dussel doing this duty in the camp. I have not seen hide nor hair of him, but this would be an easy job for him, probably with extra provisions, and he might be able to help our Annexe family from the inside. He is Jewish, but the doctor who examined my throat, front, and back is a German Jew, as best I can tell.

The bad news. Do you remember when I would tell you of a new word I had learned in my language studies? Well, I have a new word for you today, "scabies." It is a rash caused by some sort of hard-to-see mite that lives in closed quarters of prisons. They lay their eggs in the folds of the skin, bring all kinds of skin issues, and are not too contagious unless you sleep in close, unclean, flea-infested places. Translation? I have them, and I cannot go back to the barrack until I lose them.

The good news. I am in my bunk alright, but not the one I was in this morning. I am in a bunk in the scabies barrack. More good news – I can have visitors so Mother and Margot are able to check on me. Even more good news – I am getting a break from the persistent, nonsensical rock hauling.

I will be honest. I do see that God is looking out for me. I do not want scabies, but at just the right time, when I was growing weary and fearful my health would fail, I have been given a momentary reprieve. I just wish, to a degree, that Margot had scabies too, so we could be together.

Yours, Anne M. Frank

Monday, September 25, 1944

Dearest Kitty,

Another day in para-lice. Thank you for helping me joke. It is hard to be funny when so many are in misery. I have seen several naked corpses since I have been here. They are left outside after death, and they are counted at roll call until they are marked from the rolls and taken to the crematorium. I can say that now openly. We all have a good idea what goes on around here. This is a death camp.

It is clear from the circumstantial evidence. Here's what I mean. Trains come in almost every day with thousands upon thousands of people. We have no empty barracks. Every barrack here overflows. So where do they find room?

There are also thousands called for "work" duty or to be "transported." They are called up at all hours. They are marched out, yet no trains are in the yard. They never return. Not ironically, the smoke thickens at the end of this compound soon after they are led out. The older inmates who have been elevated to trustees of sorts, say they are gassed and/or shot. Then they are cremated. When we ask someone where a missing barrack mate is, they respond, "Oh, they're in the sick barracks" or "Oh, they went up the chimney." It's the latter that scares us. Sadly, the former seems to lead to the latter. I pray the scabies go away soon.

Yours, Anne M. Frank

Tuesday, September 26, 1944

My dearest Kitty,

I am still in the scabies barrack. Mother and Margot came to see me when they got off work. Our work here lasts eleven to twelve hours each day. I don't know how they have the energy to come and see me, but they come. Mother is eating. How do I know? She ate right in front of me. Now that she knows I have food, Margot has convinced her that we are fine and that she needs to eat. Margot always had a better way with Mother.

Bored silly in the sick barrack, but grateful, I have been thinking more about... I know you are sick of hearing about this, Kitty. I truly know you are. But, I was thinking more about.... Do you want to guess? That's right, who betrayed us and caused us to be in a death camp called Auschwitz? I have been contemplating this all day. I couldn't wait to tell Mother and Margot. We had to talk low so as to not incriminate people on the outside who might still be free. I told them, and now you, that I think an inadvertent suspect could be Mr. van Hoeven, our potato supplier, or more specifically his wife. Now don't get me wrong, he is (or was) a good man and I truly do not think he or his wife did it on purpose. Do you remember when Bep told us that Mrs. van Hoeven had told her that Mr. van Hoeven had been arrested for hiding Jewish people himself? Mrs. van Hoeven said they would not let him go, because he would not break under interrogation. After a few weeks of not knowing what had happened to him, she showed up and brought some supplies to Bep. I wonder if because the Mister would not talk, the Gestapo let the Missus go free so they could follow her and perhaps uncover others in hiding?

Is that not a big "Ah!" statement? Mother sure thought so. She has now given me a bigger task – get well and get us out of this camp. I told her that is my next project.

Yours, Anne

Wednesday, September 27, 1944

Dearest Kitty,

I lay silently this day. I learned from a devout Jewish lady who suffers as I do, that today is Yom Kippur. I was familiar with the holiday, but never sure when it would fall. Hanneli and her family celebrated every Jewish holiday, and they taught me so much about the traditions behind them. Lies had spent many a Yom Kippur eating with our family, while the rest of hers fasted as God had required for this sacred Day of Atonement. Pim was never one to be stringent on our holidays, especially when we were too busy hiding. Every day was Yom Kippur. Today though, I fasted. Here, nearly every day is fasting, but I particularly took time to put my fasting to good use. I prayed for God to forgive me. I confessed my sins to Him, and I asked Him to cover me. I am especially guilty of how I ridiculed and criticized Mother. God gave me a Father and a Mother who loved me, raised me, and sacrificed for me. What did I do in return? I almost reached the point of hating my mother, feeling that I would be better without her or with some other "ideal" mother. How wrong was I? I ridiculed Father and acted as if he was foolish and naïve with regard to Mother, but also relating to my love for Peter. Thoughts are sins that only God knows. Words are things that God and the people around us know. Words can be forgotten. But documenting those thoughts and words into a hurtful note raises the sin to a higher level. When I wrote Pim my letter berating him and Mother, how horribly it panged his tender heart. He saw what I felt. He heard what I felt as he read it. He thought on what I said and reread what I had stated. My sin that day, in that letter, I fear, is cemented in his mind, never to go away. "Please, God, forgive me, and help my parents to forgive me also."

I am beating myself up today, Kitty, and that is what today is for – to get it all out before God, to admit it, and to ask Him to wipe it all away. I want a clear conscience. I want to be right. With this said, I want you to know that after all that, God was so good to me today. I felt His Presence and Light around me in the darkest place on earth.

Yours, Anne M. Frank

Thursday, September 28, 1944

My dearest Kitty,

I have a new roommate. She is my old roommate from long ago. You got it! Margot has moved in with me here on the scabies' side of town. She has come down with them too, but thankfully a lighter case. Now we both are getting some food without near the trampling we have in the barracks. The beds are not clean, but there are a lot less people in them. There are no fleas, except for the ones our new residents bring. The staff gets rid of them quickly because they don't want to carry them into their homes. Oh, fleas are fine for Jews but not for Nazi personnel! Our mattresses are still straw, thin, and often smell a little mildewed, between our treatment and our sweat. This is added to the weeks and months of the same from all the people before us.

They found Margot's scabies on a health inspection, as they looked between her fingers. She had just a light plague of them. Now, if only Mother could get them. We could all be together. I have never been too concerned for her well-being. Margot and Pim are who I have sought to emulate, but Mother has really done everything we could ask and more since we got here. Her work duties have been switched. She is on some kind of cleaning detail for the moment. This is a great change. It is labor, but it is not the "back-breaking hauling rocks up and down the yard" kind of labor.

We lost a lot of acquaintances in the rock detail. The Kapos hang around us like referees in a boxing match. If one falls, they all circle around that person to see if they can count them out, end their fight, and summarily gas, shoot, and burn them. I know I sound light-hearted about this. I am not. It is just easier to talk to you about it now that I am not in the middle of it. If I return to it, I know I may be the next to fall. I am deathly afraid of the chimney. I once joked about accidentally throwing my favorite fountain pen in the fire and said it was a consolation to me that it was cremated and how I wanted to be cremated one day too. I cringe when I recount that to you. It is sickening how flippant we can be about things we don't fully understand.

They call us by our numbers for treatment – A-25237. That's what they call me. And, A-25239. That's what they call Margot. But for you, I am and will always be –

Yours, Anne M. Frank

Friday, September 29, 1944

Dearest Kitty,

I am ready to get out of this place. The quickest way to the chimney is to become a burden in this place or in the sick barracks. Unfortunately, we cannot be released until one of their pseudo-doctors say we can. I want to leave this place, but I do not want to go back to the rock formation. We had a young girl come through here to check on her mother. She is a little older than me. She must be from France because she speaks the French language fluently to her mother. I am so glad that Father and Mother pushed us in our studies. The nurses here don't seem to understand what these two are saying, but because of my studies, I understood full-well what she was saying.

She has been able to land a job outside the wire as a nannie for one of the SS troops. They pick her up from her barracks every morning, take her to this man's home where she cleans, cooks, and watches after the kids. She gets extra food rations for doing this. She gets to shower every day. She has toothpaste and soap, and a much nicer uniform. She eats well, too, when she stays overnight in this family's home. What's even more wonderful, she is able to bring food for her mother and aunt under her dress. She was sharing all these niceties with her mother quietly. She never realized that, as I pretended to count the flies on the ceiling, I was understanding every word.

This girl helps other prisoners who do the guard's yard. She gets information about the war. She can pass notes from family members outside to family members inside. That's the job I want. Margot had been napping. When this young girl left, I told her all about this. I never knew there were such jobs available. We are both young. We are both girls. We speak Dutch, English, French, German, and have partial knowledge of others. We would be perfect for this. We can also help them with their homework. After all, we just got out of a two-year educational boot-camp a few months ago. We decided to ask Mother, the next time she came to see us, what she could find out. We would do the same.

Yours, Anne M. Frank

Saturday, September 30, 1944

Dearest Kitty,

You almost lost me today. I am still shaking at the thought. Mengele ordered that all barracks be emptied for a health inspection. Now, we are in the scabies barracks and next to us, in the infirmary, are the sick. You would think our health has already been inspected and found wanting. We all, the whole camp, had to leave our rags in the barracks and stand at attention naked in front of the watchful eyes of every soldier, doctor, Mengele, and his lieutenants. It turned out not to be so funny.

It was a selection that lasted all day. Women, young and old, were being divided again to the left and to the right. Those to the left walked down the fence row. We knew why. It's so scary that no one objects. Those to the right don't object because they don't want to be put to the left. Those to the left don't object because they have nothing left within them with which to object. They figure it doesn't matter anyway.

They came to the sick barrack first, and the vast majority were sent to the left. They left the camp for eternity. They came to our barracks. Kitty, several ahead of me were sent to the left. Margot was sent to the right. I was next. I stood as tall as I could and even covered any wince as they inspected my unclothed body. He pointed my skinny frame to the left. Margot gasped. The lab assistant behind him, ordered, "Give me your number!." He was going to write it down in his book, or mark it out from his book. I am not sure which. As a reflex, I was about to give my number, "A-252..." But the head officer had already pointed to the three behind me to go to the left. At that moment, they all ran for the electric fence several meters away. The guards all chased after them. They would not have this chicken-chasing in the camp. They drew their guns to fire, but before they could, the women reached the fence. There was a burning, a sizzle, a muted scream, some convulsing, and death.

I was horrified, but I realized there were no guards near me. The one who was going to write down my number had dropped his book and chased after the women. I saw my chance and slid over into the line on the right. I had lost sight of Margot, but I knew she was there somewhere. Other women pulled me in, and placed themselves as a wall between me and the guards just in case they would recognize me. The commotion and the tragedy had served its purpose. Those to the left, who remained, marched to their gassing. We, to the right, marched back to the scabies barrack. There I was restored to Margot. We were both resolved; we must get out of this barrack quickly and post-haste. I pray there is never another close call like this.

Yours, the almost Late Anne M. Frank

Monday, October 2, 1944

Dearest Kitty,

Margot and I are back in our barrack 29 with Mother. My first thought was to tell you we were back home, but I will never, ever call this place home, not even in jest. Barrack 29 may be where we are staying for now. I will never say I live there, and I will never call it home. They say home is where the heart is. My heart is not here. My loved ones are here, at least two of them. I grieve at the thought that my three loved ones may have been reduced to two. As I was saying, my loved ones' hearts are not here either. Our hearts are somewhere in Holland or Switzerland. Not here. We were released yesterday by one of the doctors after saying the mites and eggs were dead and our clothes had been boiled. We are clean, though our clothes fit a little tighter which is good considering we are smaller now than before.

Roll call came early this morning. Actually, it was the normal time, but I had been out of action for a blessed week and Margot for a few days. Mother was called back to her cleaning job. Margot and I now have the privilege to shovel dirt. We dug holes today, and it seems we will be digging holes in the foreseeable future. Maybe these holes will eventually become a trench. We do not know their plans. They tell us it is none of our business what we are doing. If they say dig, the guards say we are to dig. If they say move rocks from one end to the other, we are to move rocks from one end to the other. We then are told to move the rocks back from whence they came, so we do. It is horrific work, much worse than the battery job we had in Westerbork. There they were nicer to us, but the logic of all this free labor going toward this type of stuff makes no sense at all. Their sort of logic is going to lose them the war. Or, so I hope.

Some of these guards seem like they are prisoners in their own right. The vast majority of them don't seem happy either. They get berated by the person ahead of them in rank. That person gets lambasted by the person over him. I would like to ask them all, "Why are we doing this to each other? Can't we just all go home and live normal, love-filled lives? Let us live, and then live our lives, so you can go back to living yours." Surely no one but the Fuhrer had this sort of life envisioned for themselves when they dreamed as children. Won't someone stand up? Anybody? If not a Nazi, how about an SS man? If not an SS man, how about a German? If not a German, why won't a Polish citizen who lives just beyond our wire do something? Don't get me wrong. I am told there is resistance even in this country, but why so few and where are they? If we could just stand together, evil would be outnumbered, outgunned, and outmanned.

Yours, Anne M. Frank

Tuesday, October 3, 1944

Dearest Kitty,

I should be feeling stronger after my week-long vacation on the continent of scabies-land, but I am not. Maybe I am getting flabby and out of shape, I don't know. Margot seems to be fine. Mother is doing well. But, I am not. I pray to God this passes. I want to be strong and plucky Anne again.

We got in a few hours ago, had our piece of bread, a small bucket of soup we shared, and we each got a potato. We must have a new chef in this fine establishment! We got in our bunks. The dust from the bunk above me choked me down. I was getting all settled in, lights were still on, and Sarah, a German Jew sat up three bunks down and said, "I am tired of being a number!" I have been one for so long, morning and night, and at every work detail, I have almost forgotten who I am. That gave me an idea.

"Ladies, I know you're tired, but can we play a short game? I just thought of this. We will call it the game of 'Who am I?' I will begin it and then whoever wants to share can follow me. Just raise your hand. We will take ten people tonight before the lights go off." Margot was laying on her side. She flipped to her stomach on the middle bunk of a stacked three bunk construction. Her arms were under her, with her hands holding onto the side wooden rail. I was excited to see who would play this game. I wanted to see their faces, hear their names, and see what they would say about themselves.

I began, "Who am I? I am Annelies Marie Frank. I go by Anne. I am the daughter of Otto and Edith Frank, sister of Margot Frank. I am in love with two Peters and cannot make up my mind which I like best. I love to read. I hate maths. My best friend for the last almost three years is Kitty. She is not here, but I am sure she is doing great. I want to be a famous writer." Everyone applauded with smiles. Just then, our Kapo, an inmate leader of our barracks, known for being blistering tough walked in. We got quiet. She could tell there was an edge in the room, brought on by her entrance. She smiled and said, "I am sorry for being the way I have been. Please, will you continue? Understand, I am a prisoner like you, facing the same fate. I didn't ask for this job, but they have my family. We all, at that moment, understood that each person here, from the inmates on up to the guards has a story that could explain the actions we are seeing.

Everyone looked at me, the youngest in a bunk. I smiled at her. Her name was Gisela. I said, "Welcome Gisela. We are playing a game. Feel free to join in when you are comfortable." Just then, I saw Freda's hand go up, so I asked, "Who are you?" She answered, "Who am I? I am Freda Gayle Schneider. I am the daughter of Charles and Hilda Schneider. My mom is a hard worker at an office. My dad? I don't know for sure what he does during the day, but when he's home, he puts his feet on the footstool, breaks wind from his behind, and gives orders." We all laughed. "I want to one day be Freda Goldman by marrying a sweet guy from our village named Fredrich. I only want kids if he will give them birth!." There was great applause again and laughter. This was fun.

A few others took their turn. We were past our curfew for the lights, but Gisela let them linger. After some very innovative and interesting answers, I could not believe what I saw. Gisela's hand went up. I asked her, "Who are you?" Gisela was nervously hesitating, but wanting to join the fun, she answered, "Who am I? I am Gisela Donie Fields, a teacher at the university in Berlin. I am Jewish. I am the daughter of Abraham and Elizabeth. I have a husband named Seth. He is an engineer. We have a nice home, but no children yet. We hope to one day have three sons, two daughters, and a cat." People chuckled at the "cat." I could not help but speak up, "We have fleas, but no cat. That's what's been missing!" Gisela smiled, "Alright then."

Before we could get to the next person, a whistle sounded, and Gisela said, "We better turn the lights off." We all booed in play, but not too loudly. If one person gets the guard mad, we all suffer. We have learned that. We had a good night, Kitty, and I was glad to talk about you to other people. I am just glad they didn't ask more about you. Dr. Mengele might want to do a study of my mental state.

Yours, Anne M. Frank

Wednesday, October 4, 1944

Dearest Kitty,

Today has been a bear. My stomach hurt all day and I had toilet issues, as you can imagine, as a result. I don't know if I got some bad turnip soup last night, or perhaps there is a bug going around. There are plenty of bugs going around, I might add. Needless to say, I didn't carry my load, but Mother and Margot stayed on each side of me and helped.

I think what got me through the day was the game "Who am I?" It seems to have carried on into the day. Anytime we would hear a number called out, and the person responded and did whatever they were told, another from our barrack would begin quietly saying, "Who am I? I am Liddy Wagner. I am the daughter of...." It was such a good answer to what we have been feeling. No matter what number they mark us with, no matter how poorly they treat us, we are human beings. I am a person. I have a name. I have a family. I have feelings. I cannot tell you how that lightened my heart.

I must have made an impact on Gisela. At our evening feeding, Gisela came to me after our distribution and gave me some extra bread when no one was looking. I was about to say thank you, but she put her index finger to her lips to silence me and smiled. What a blessing. God has not left me here. He has given us friends and favor, even here in the depths of our earthly Hell.

Yours, I am Annelies Marie Frank

Thursday, October 5, 1944

My dearest Kit,

You will never guess who came to visit me today? I will give you a hint – it is the visitor that I had longed to see for a long time, and when she came I was so happy. Any guess? I knew I would stump you with that. My period came today. I always wanted to have them because they were a sign that I was a woman. When I had my first one, I was so thrilled. As you know, they have not been real regular, but more often than not, they came each month, except here. This is my first one since we arrived. It seems many of the women had theirs when they first got here and then stopped having them. The ladies who have some medical background say it is because of the stress and lack of nutrients and vitamins. If that's the case, I should not be having mine. But here it came. Thankfully, while we were in scabies barrack, I had the foresight to take some napkins just in case. What a smart girl Anne is!

I am hoping this was why my stomach was hurting yesterday. I still feel like I have a lingering rash, but Margot is all clear, and I had it worse than she did. I will keep an eye on it. I was able to work today and carry a little more of my load.

Yours, Anne M. Frank

Friday, October 6, 1944

My dearest Kitty,

Our resident religious expert, Margot, brought to my attention that we are in the midst of Sukkot, the Feast of Tabernacles. She can be so humorous in her own pointy-headed way. She told me what it meant, as if I had not grown up in a Jewish family. My best friend, after all, was of the most devout Jewish family that we knew. Hanneli and I had shared many a Jewish holiday at her house. Every Sukkot, I would go to their home and sit in their booth and eat a meal with them. I even helped decorate their booth. The Goslars had no concept of proper décor. Besides, her dad was kind of a downer. He seemed so religious that he could not enjoy the life he had been given.

I don't know why Margot is always reminding me of things I already know. It is extremely irritating, but such things kid sisters have to put up with, I suppose. If only Pim and Mother would have had another baby for me to entertain with my knowledge. However, if it makes Margot feel better, very well then. She said, "You know Anne, this is the Feast of Tabernacles. Just to remind you, this is the week we are to live in booths outside our homes and remember our forefathers who were in the desert wilderness for forty years. They were caught between slavery and the Promised Land. They made it the best they could and God provided for them, though the people constantly rebelled even in affliction."

I piped in, "How appropriate is that! We are not in our homes. We are in the wilderness I guess, but I feel more like we are still in Egypt, greatly oppressed. And, truly the natives are grumbling, even among themselves." Margot interrupted, "Not so in our barrack Anne! I think God is pleased with our group." I smiled and agreed with her fully.

I can't wait to be set free. Where is our Moses? Where is our Joshua?

Yours, Anne M. Frank

Saturday, October 7, 1944

My Kitty,

There was a fight in the barracks across from us this evening. We heard alarms sound, trucks came pulling up, guards with guns, and dogs making horrible sounds. The dust settled, the quite was returned. We had no idea what was going on because we were all told not to look out. They didn't have to tell us. We were afraid to look out anyway.

I am so glad about the barrack that we are in. We have some very kind people here in the "Who am I" dorm. They are making our lives a little nicer as a community. Some barracks are at total war. When their doors are closed and lights are ordered off, fights ensue over windows being opened or closed, over who is hogging the blanket, or settling a score over who took a spoon or a piece of bread. We hear they argue over people getting up in the middle of the night to go to the latrine. We often have to crawl over each other and awaken weary bodies who had just drifted to sleep, after much worry and crying. There are some things for which to be thankful. I have people who love me and still care for me. And I have you, Kitty, to relieve my stress and to listen to my cries and concerns.

Yours, Anne M. Frank

Sunday, October 8, 1944

My dearest Kitty,

I want to tell you about an odd noise I had forgotten to tell you about in our barrack. It started several Sundays ago, just as the lights had been turned off. The first Sunday I noticed it, there was just this slender, weak voice mumbling something almost as if an old poem or quotation. I could not tell what she was saying, but the next Sunday, as soon as the lights went out, I heard it again. Most of us kept talking on our side of the barrack, but soon we heard, "Shhhh!" carry across this cavernous, yet packed, stalag. I thought maybe a guard was coming, so we got quiet and waited. No one came. The next Sunday, lights went out, and we were almost expecting it. There it was. But this time, there were more saying it with this person. Some were in unison, but I still could not make it out. Because it began and ended so soon after the lights were out, and because we were all tired, it didn't make enough of an impression for me to ask questions the next morning.

This past Sunday night, just after the lights were turned off, I was waiting for it. It is almost like catching a firefly on a summer night. You just catch the glimpse of one, or so you think. You wait, hold still, looking in the place you thought you saw it, just to see another flash, but in an unexpected distance away. You then widen your view, and silently you wait. Then you catch it. Maybe it was a firefly, or maybe it was many. The more you hone in, the more you are able to spot them; your eyes adjust, and you have the joy of watching the orchestra of flickers. That's what this was like. I waited and kept still. It began, but this time, even more joined in, and they were saying it almost in one voice in German, French, Dutch, and Italian, "Our Father who art in Heaven, hallowed be Thy Name. Thy Kingdom come. Thy Will be done on earth as it is in Heaven. Give us this day our daily bread and forgive us our trespasses as we forgive those who trespass against us. And lead us not into temptation, but deliver us from evil. For Thine is the Kingdom and the Power and the Glory forever. Amen." It was just beautiful.

I asked one of the ladies, the next day, to tell me where it was found. She said it was the Lord's Prayer from the New Testament. It had a ring of familiarity from some of the prayers in the Old Testament, but nowhere near as concise and complete as this one. I asked her to teach it to me and she did in between work detail. Mother, who always loved our prayer times, learned it along with Margot and me.

Just now, we were ready. We all three, in our bed of eight, sat in rapt attention. The lights went out. Here it comes...."Our Father who art in Heaven..." We joined in right away. There were more of us than ever before. Some, of course, were irritated. Some, even in our bunk, covered their ears. There were a lot of once religious people in this room who now were atheist. They said there is no way God would allow this. And, they said if there is a God and He allows this suffering, then they will have no part in Him. I understand the doubts and anger, but I don't blame God for this. I know He has always been with me. I believe in eternal life, and I believe in an eternal death which is far worse than what we are facing. The fires at the end of this block can't touch what I believe of the eternal fire. Margot was more familiar with the background on this than I was.

Pim had always wanted to get me a copy of the New Testament. He had even talked to Mr. Kugler about getting me one a few Christmases ago. Now I wish he would have. I think of the suffering we are going through as Jews and I realize that Jesus, who was a Jew, suffered too. We are innocent, held guilty just for who we are – Jews. Jesus was innocent, held guilty for who He was. I have got to learn more. Pim had always said that Jesus was a perfect example of how to handle hard times, difficult people, and of how to love no matter what befalls us. I see little reason to love in this place; and yet, I see love in this place.

They said it again; the first time they ever did it twice. I joined in, "Our Father who art in Heaven, hallowed by Thy Name. Thy Kingdom come. Thy Will be done on earth as it is in Heaven. Give us this day our daily bread and forgive us our trespasses as we forgive those who trespass against us. And lead us not into temptation, but deliver us from evil. For Thine is the Kingdom and the Power and the Glory forever. Amen." It just made us feel so much better. He wants us to love. He wants peace. He wants all to be treated with respect. That is His Will. So tonight, we are praying for that Will of His to be done here in Auschwitz, in Poland, in Germany. So we can go home.

Yours, Anne M. Frank

Monday, October 9, 1944

My dearest Kitty,

I am so thankful for last night. Today was grueling, and I don't think I could have made it without last night. Do you remember me telling you about the day we arrived here? I saw a mother and her children walking toward the end of our camp, being reassured of schools, work, and time together at the end of the day. Those children were exhausted, but almost skipping holding their mother's hands, one on each side. Of course, we thought that was all a lie, and we never did see those people again. I have cried most of the day, thinking of that little family and the many who have come after them.

We have been here over a month now, and we are more than aware of what goes on just at the end of this complex. Gisela gave me the most descriptive explanation I have ever heard this morning after roll call. Some new transports came in, and the same scene was played out between the male and female sections of the camp, where the train tracks run and the cars unload. Those who are sent to the left go through the most horrifying thing I have ever heard. Gisela says those people, perhaps the majority having an idea that what happens next won't be good, still remain hopeful for the best. Many are encouraged by the SS troops to prevent panic or a run for the gate. They are taken to the very end of Auschwitz, the end of the world for them. They see a long building where they are walked to the end of it, through an entrance into a huge spacious changing room. They are told to disrobe – old and young, children and adults. Of course, the family is trying to stay together. The guards stand on both ends watching.

They tell them to hang their clothes on the hooks, leaving their valuables in their purses and pockets. Each hook has a number. They are told to remember that number so that after the delousing, they will have no trouble finding their things. They are told a guard will watch their things to make sure nothing is taken. Uncomfortably, but obediently, they all disrobe. The room is filled with naked people. Parents try to shield their children. Adults try to look ahead instead of at each other's bodies. Children look around, but mainly up to hold their parents' eyes. Invariably, some children will ask their mothers, "Why are they doing this to us, Mommy?" That is the question, isn't it?

Why are they doing this after all? There is no answer other than hatred and evil. I cannot get my head around one human being doing this to another. You may say, well it is not just one human being, it is many human beings doing this to other human beings. That is too broad for the truth. The truth is, they are not doing this as a mass of people who are unfeeling and oblivious, as if what is done by them can't be seen by them. If someone runs over an individual in an automobile, there is some excuse, "Well, I didn't see them. They ran out in front of me." That is possible. But, this? Each SS soldier, independently and individually, commits these atrocious acts. And they are doing it not to just some group of people, but to individual people – sons, daughters, mothers, fathers, brothers, sisters. Though we all take the punishment or death with others, we each suffer and/or die individually. That is what drives home to me the evil of man. I would love to see that each person has some good in them, and maybe they do toward their own family members. But, there is evil in their hearts to do this, to let these things happen, to watch, and to participate. There is covering in the crowd of offenders, but no lessening of the guilt.

After all have been stripped naked, they are then led to another room with fake showerheads. They are told to be ready when the water is turned on. They are to receive the disinfectant on themselves first, and then they are to ensure that their children are disinfected fully afterward. These instructions sound too descript to be anything but an honest to goodness disinfecting. They think, "Maybe we aren't going to die like we thought. Maybe these Germans really are trying to prevent disease." In the "shower room", these recent arrivals into the camp try to remember their hook number and the instructions for delousing. They can't wait to get back to their clothes. The doors are shut. The lights suddenly go out. Then a drop is heard in two parts of the big room where they have been moved. A horrible odor starts to emanate. The smell is toxic and breathing is hard. They begin to scream from panic, trying to get to higher ground, to climb over each other to get out. Mothers are weeping as they try to hold on to their kids in the darkness, but lose their hands in the suffocating fumes. They cover their noses and faces in reflex; then reaching back, they try but can no longer find the little hand of their child. They call, but there is too much screaming to hear. It is the most heinous of chaotic killings. The chemical used to kill insects is used to kill Jews.

It is all over in minutes. Gisela with tears in her eyes, tells me these things while I am weeping in disbelief. She says well-fed and clothed Jewish prisoners called the Sonderkommando let the gases evaporate and then they enter. They pull the gold out of the teeth of the victims. They shave the heads to use the hair for textiles. They put the corpses on carts several at a time and incinerate the remains. In a few hours, a whole train load goes "up the chimney." Life over. They never have the opportunity to answer the significant question, "Who am I?" No one but family, if they survive, will know.

Yours, Anne M. Frank

Tuesday, October 10, 1944

Dearest Kitty,

It was a restless sleep last night. It's not because we have no pillows in this place. I have gotten accustomed to using my arms and hands folded together for my pillow. It wasn't the fleas last night, as I have become very acclimated to them. It wasn't even the people crawling over us to go to the latrine. I have been able to sleep through that in my exhaustion from the day's labor.

So, what was it? Every time I closed my eyes and began to enter the safety of sleep, my friend Hanneli would appear in my dreams like she did back in the Annexe. Do you remember those dreams I told you about? They are all so similar. Hanneli is in rags, frail, thin, and in anguish. I can tell by the way she speaks to me that she is distraught. I hear the roar of a burning fire all around her. I see people dying to her left and right. She is trying to stand still while being knocked around by the brute beasts chasing, whipping, and killing the people around her. With the saddest of expressions, she looks into my eyes with a terrible accusing hurt, as if I have been doing nothing to assist her. Hanneli is pleading with me again to help her.

When I first had this dream, we were safely kept away in the Annexe. I had no idea what to make of that dream. Now that I am here in the death camp, I am wearing the clothes Hanneli was wearing. I have that same frail, thin condition, and I am in anguish. I try so hard to ignore it, to have hope, to keep myself upbeat so that others will find some light in this place. But I am silently crying myself to sleep most nights, dying on the inside as people are dying on the outside. I do not know if Hanneli is alive or if she is facing this. Maybe she is in this camp or has gone through here. I saw Hanneli in my dream, or was I seeing me all along? With the hair shaved and the prison rags, it is hard to tell who anyone is.

My sleep is often disturbed most nights any way by the sounds of trucks moving through our barracks, by screams, gun shots, doors slamming, guards shouting, or dogs growling. With these occurrences, we just keep our heads down and watch our door to see if they are coming to take us away. So far, they haven't. But how long, really, does anyone have here? I am unnerved and losing my composure. Part of me just wants to run out screaming, throw myself onto the wire, and to join the skull and crossbones sign as a warning.

Yours, Anne M. Frank

Wednesday, October 11, 1944

Dearest Kitty,

Another roll call. Another medical check-up. Another selection. They took away eighteen of our barrack family this morning. A woman that Mother had known from her youth, named Tamara, was escorted past our rank and file when her number was called. Mother is heartbroken. She looked at Mother as she walked by, nodded her head, mouthed, "I am ready", and strolled boldly by.

I am starting to understand the words, "I am ready." We are beaten and bruised every day. The Nazis, the SS troops, the Kapos, and fellow prisoners all take part in this deconstructing escapade. When we were living in the freedom of Amsterdam, I often wanted to leave my parents and be free to live on my own. Then we went into the Annexe. It was great at first, like a camp-out. We fought for two years not to get caught. We held our silence, modified our activities, and lived life only when others weren't living theirs. It grew old and, before long, we all toyed with the idea that getting caught might not be so bad. At least it would be over. We would be free one way or the other. Then we got caught. The old adage, "Be careful what you wish for" sure applied to us. Now, we have been spending all our time trying to stay alive. I have to be honest, and this sentiment permeates much of our camp, dying may be the relief we long for. At the least, this would all be over.

If Pim were alive, I would love to see him. He would give me hope. On the other hand, if Pim was killed in the nightmare of the gas chamber when we arrived, I could consider him lucky for three reasons. One, he doesn't have to see all this agony. Two, he doesn't have to suffer any more. And three, he doesn't have to worry about us. If Father is alive, he may wonder if we are dead. He may grieve at night wondering what we are going through and how can he help us. If Father were alive, he would probably be second guessing himself, thinking he could have done things better. If Father is alive today, I hope he is taking care of Peter. I hope he and Mr. Van Daan are working together. If Father is alive, I can imagine he has touched some lives among the captives and among the captors alike. I can imagine things are better wherever Pim is.

Yours, Anne M. Frank

Thursday, October 12, 1944

Dearest Kitty,

If you were writing a diary to me, what would you be saying?

Dearest Anne,

I have graduated from the 12th form. I now have a job and am dating a sweet young man named Liam. He loves me and has a great sense of humor. He loves to walk outside in the cool of the evening, holding my hand and visiting about everything under the sun. Liam wants to marry me, but he hasn't built up the courage to ask my father. He knows that he needs to be able to provide for me. Though he is ready to marry now, it will be a few years before he can save enough money to provide us a place to live and some furniture to sit on I tell him all the time that I am in no hurry. If my life progresses just like this without any change, I will be happy. I have my family and my love. What more do I need?

Liam is always wondering what I am writing to you, Anne. He wonders if I am talking about him. You know better. He reminds me in some ways of what Peter could be if he would ever grow up. Liam thinks it odd that I never miss a day of writing my thoughts to you. I tell him that it is my way of coping in this world. I remind him that you and I have a friendship that is so deep and valuable that no one will ever be able to understand. He says he wants to be that to me. I tell him what you always tell me. It's hard to open up with people you live with or those who are around you every day. Some things are better not said, but worked out with outside, objective parties.

He has seen me weep over your letters. I am so worried about you Anne. I pray for you. I hang on every word you send me. I am overwhelmed that in your distress and torture, you are able to be so strong, to lead others in your barrack, and bear the physical toll along with the mental anguish. I cannot live a day without hearing from you. When you don't write (or speak), I fear that I have lost you. Anne, we are one. Just as you say that I am a help to you, you are a help to me. I wish I could share your words with others. I know they would be as touched as I am. But trust me, your words are safe with me. Keep them coming!

Yours always, Kitty

Sorry for the pause, Kitty. I just took a moment to think of what a letter from you might say. You are a great help to me, and I thank you so much for being there. I hope your life is going much better than mine. I was walking to our work station outside today, though there is death all around. The smell and ugliness of this place seems to discourage any plant from growing or any bird from singing. Nevertheless, as I was walking, the breeze seemed to change. At some distance, there must be a rain on a farmer's field. It was the sweetest smell I have had in a long time. It caught me totally by surprise. It was real. It was sharp. And, it was exquisite. I began to walk slower. I held my nose up, breathed deeply in, hoping to catch another whiff. It was hard, but three or four times I was able to capture it in my nostrils and draw it deeply into my lungs, even deeper into my being. That is the smell of creation. That is the smell of freedom. That is the smell that I believe God has given to me. Do you value that aroma, Kitty? Please do.

Your always, Anne

Friday, October 13, 1944

Dearest Kitty,

A cold wind blew into our barracks today. Yes, Fall is approaching. No, it wasn't Fall. It was Mengele. There have been so many transports coming in and our camp is overflowing with people. Nearly everyone who dismounted from the train were pointed to the left line. All the men and women and boys and girls arriving throughout the day were taken to the end of the world. The fire blew hot. The smell grew strong. The smoke engulfed even the inside of our barracks. I wish the cremma would blow. There is talk that the Sonderkammondo might try that one day. They are nearing their four-month tenure which is bad for them.

As if that wasn't enough, we were ordered at roll call to medical check-up which means enhanced selection. We went to our barracks, took off our clothes, and then lined back up. I wonder what the new arrivals thought walking to their doom, "Why is everyone standing outside naked in rank?" Mengele had help, but this time my company went directly under his eye. Five by five we stood before him. Five by five, he did his exam. One by one, he made his decision. He let Mother go, but stopped Margot and me as we walked briskly by him trying to stick with Mother. He talked sweet and showed great concern. He was like a younger grandfather. This is the Mengele we have learned about. He acts like an angel from Heaven, yet he turns into the angel of death. The Bible says, per one of our Christian roommates, that Satan can masquerade as an angel of light. I believe that wholeheartedly.

But I digress. Mengele saw that my rash had returned and sent me straight to the infirmary. He thought he saw some places on Margot's body, but he told her he would check her again in a few days. I was kind of glad to get to go back to the infirmary. My body was so worn-out. Though Gisela had given me extra food when she was our Kapo, she has now been reassigned to another camp. Needless to say, we have been doing without like every other prisoner here. Mother, again, has been giving us her food. She has been very open about it with us. If anyone gets chosen in our family for the selection, she is making sure that it will be her. She says this makes sense because we are her legacy. She is unable to be ours. We argue with her, but you know how Mother is!

I knew my way to the scabies holding cell, but a female guard led me and a few others. We walked in. Everything had changed. Obviously, there was a new commander in town. It was darker than before and dirtier than ever. I saw three rats pause when we entered. Not one of them feared enough to flee. The rats watched us come in just as easily as our sick partners. I had recovered in this place not too long ago, as had my peers. But gauging by those here, one comes in here sick just to get sicker still. I was assigned a mat on the floor. There was no straw, nor a wooden slat of a bed this time. People were crying from thirst. They wanted to know if we had any extra bread in our pockets. They offered us paper money, but what good would that do us here? I saw a woman the other day rip up her guilders into three parts to use for toilet paper. All our valuables were taken at the Annexe. We had nothing to barter when we arrived, and have very little with which to do that now.

I should be thankful. The vast majority of people Mengele examined today headed to the end of our complex. The smoke continued to fill the sky to the point it seemed the atmosphere could hold no more. Mother and Margot cleared selection. I did too in a different route, but for how long?

Yours, Anne M. Frank

Saturday, October 14, 1944

Well Kit,

I never thought you would hear me say this, but I think the work detail of moving rocks is better than this. It stinks in here. I am dying of thirst. I am itching all over. It seems the mites from my neighbors are having baby mites who are making apartments all over my body. I have become a colony of eggs and little ones. My itching and rash will have to be my proof because I cannot see the little buggers. I try to take this lightly Kitty, but who am I fooling. I don't have to be strong for you. I don't have to put on a face for you. I am miserable. I can't rest. I am filthy, hungry, and thirsty. Beyond that, no one can come see me. It is as if I have entered the waiting room for death. We can almost hear them emptying the carts and putting more coals and wood on the fire as they turn to walk our way.

Mother has been hard at work. She has become very ingenious in this place and has networked quite well. She and another lady have dug a hole under the wall and they are getting food to me. What a blessing! How she loves me. If I could rewrite my diary to you Kit, I would mark out so many of the awful things I was saying. I believed they were true at the moment, but no one has the foresight to see how people change, and no one has the insight to see what others are on the inside. I am fed. I chew quietly, so that no one attacks me or reports Mother and her helper.

I pray to get well Kitty. How can I get well if I don't sleep? And, how can I sleep if the itching doesn't stop? How can my itching stop if they don't or won't get rid of my scabies?

Yours, Anne M. Frank

Sunday, October 15, 1944

It was a lonely and dark day today. I hear more are being killed beyond these walls. I also heard some nurses talking. They said the whole of the sick barracks was emptied yesterday into the gas chamber. They felt they had dealt with these people enough. How long until they do the same with us?

I remember being in that Annexe and having to be quiet. Any time someone would be brought into the office below us, we would listen intently to find out what they were doing and to see if our fate was involved. How little did we realize the value of that skill for our future? Now we all listen intently. Our lessons in languages are paying off. We act as if we don't understand half of what we hear. This helps people to speak more freely in front of us.

What I am hearing is not good. The war is going great for our side, but the delays are literally killing us in this camp. What little light there is in this place has been turned off. They have ordered us to sleep. I don't know how you order anyone to sleep. It's not something we do on command, but they obviously think they can speak that into obedience as well.

Lights are out. Do you know what I miss most? Mother? Yes and no. Margot? Yes and no. What I miss most? I miss that one voice starting it off on Sunday night when the lights went out. That growing wave of that prayer we prayed every night in our private bunker, "Our Father who art in Heaven, hallowed by Thy Name. Thy Kingdom come. Thy Will be done on earth as it is in Heaven. Give us this day our daily bread and forgive us our trespasses as we forgive those who trespass against us. And lead us not into temptation, but deliver us from evil. For Thine is the Kingdom and the Power and the Glory forever. Amen." I said it by myself here in the scabies quarters, but no one joined me. That's okay. I did it anyway and I feel better. Kitty I need you to confide in, but you and I both know that you are powerless to help. That's where that prayer comes in handy. I know God can help me. I will trust in Him.

Yours, Anne

Monday, October 16, 1944

My dearest Kitty,

You are not going to believe this! If another had not confirmed it, I would not have believed it either. There was a transport today. The Germans are needing laborers for one of their plants. The offer was good food, clean clothes, hard work, and more freedom. It sounded just like any other ruse they give us. This is why no one readily volunteers for these duties unless they are just so fed up with the mess that they decide either death or work would be better than this place.

What made this offer so believable was an empty train pulled in. They were taking people out of here. If they were going to kill people, chances are there would have been no train, but just a promise of a train. We have all believed that if we can just get out of the death camp, we might be able to live to the end of the war. Mother and Margot were offered a chance to go on this train. They are both good workers and neither of them have had any disciplinary issues. Besides, Mother is so connected here, she could probably write her own ticket.

Do you know what they did? They said, "No. Not until Anne can go with us." Can you believe that? They didn't come in to tell me. Of course, they can't come in. The lady, who carries my bread from Mother and places it into the Anne Frank hole beneath the infirmary wall, slid a note inside my piece of bread. She was telling me what Mother and Margot did. How could they pass that chance? Would I have? I think so. I think

Pim built that into us. We Franks stick together – in a house, in an Annexe, in a work camp, and in a death camp.

I cannot wait to get my hands on those nearly-bald, totally skinny
women. I am going to wring their necks as I hug them both so tightly.

Yours, Anne Frank

Tuesday, October 17, 1944

Dearest Kitty,

In our old barrack, the one where Mother and Margot have chosen
to stay because of me, the ladies in our section had drawn a calendar on
the wall. Together we remember what day it is in the morning and we
check the day off in the evening. I don't know whose idea that was exactly, but it is a practice that you and I have been carrying out for quite a
while. In this captivity of ours, no day has any significance and there is
no particular date in which to look forward to in the future.

When I was younger, I looked forward to my birthday, or to Hanukkah, or even to Christmas. We loved celebrating Father's birthday, Margot's birthday, or going to see Grandma. In life before Hitler, it seemed I
was living from one day to the next, always looking forward to some
eventful day. It was always the next closest event that got me through
the days I lived between. I was able to get through one school year looking forward to the day our grades came back, and we could move onto
the next level at school. But now, we just live each day. There is no ex-
citement about this day or the next day; much less, a thought of the next
week. Each day is filled only with dread. Even today, there is barely a
distant hope. We seldom allow ourselves to think of a day in the future
where the war will end and we will be set free. Why not let ourselves
look to that day? Because with each day where that does not occur, we

are plunged deeper into depression. We live from one drab, sad day to another. We are spectators and victims in a world where the so-called "inferior" race gets beaten down by the SS's self-acclaimed "superior" race. To them, the only difference between us and the roaches is the amount of effort it takes to kill either. This is a world of evolution, where the strong survive. I want to live in the world of creation, where God created the heavens and the earth, and formed each person in the womb of their mothers, giving each of us breath, life, value, and identity. I want to live in the world where God alone gives us life, and as Solomon wrote, God alone determines when this life given graduates to the next life eternal. Truly even now, I know our future still rests in His Hand, not the Fuhrer's.

There are no calendars in this scabies barrack anyway. There is a date here that we long for, which is the date we can get out of here. Sickbed wasn't so bad in times past. It was a place of cleanliness, food, rest, and recovery. They have turned this place into a place where even the sickest prefer not to go. What makes things worse? I fear the sound of each arriving train. Not just for the ones being brought here, but for the ones having to leave through the chimney at the tracks' end. Every set of footsteps I hear coming down this dank hallway, I fear belong to Mengele. How long until he decides treatment is no longer an option for me? This is my second trip here. When will he think in his wicked mind that I am a liability, a vector of this plague. I am Jewish after all.

Yours, Anne M. Frank

Wednesday, October 18, 1944

Dearest Kitty,

If not for Mother! Can you believe I am saying that? I know. I hear you. You have been with me a long time, but it is true. She is the most resourceful, enterprising woman I have ever known. At times, I wonder if she runs this camp. She gets me food. She is able to get it to me past so many barriers. She negotiates, cuts deals, and forms a working pipeline: an underground railroad of sorts.

I have always thought that the female gender could stand side-by-side with the male gender and reach even greater heights if given the chance. My beliefs have been realized in the form of "MY" mother. Did you catch that Kitty? I called Mrs. Edith Frank my mother. I gladly lay claim to her.

Father was great at business. He could create a business, run a business, and manage the resources, including the manpower. He drew adoration, an income, and a loyal following as seen in Kleinman, Kugler, Voskuijl , Miep, Bep, Van Daan, and more. As many great resources as Father had personally and corporately, he missed taking advantage of perhaps his greatest resource – Mother. What a team they would have made.

Yours, Anne M. Frank

Thursday, October 19, 1944

The train pulled in this morning. I didn't see it, but I heard it. I also heard the selections going on in the street. There was fear, a little resistance (very little), tearful goodbyes, and wailing. The wailing was silenced by a thud, a soldier's warning, and a march either to the rock pile or to the gas chamber. I am not sure which way the marching I heard went.

Billows of smoke blew into our dark hospital floor, which is where I lay. The smell was so nauseating. It would be no matter what, but it is worse when I know who they are burning - fathers and mothers, sisters and brothers, sons and daughters. They kill, kill, and kill some more. What do they do with all those bodies? They burn and bury, but more burn than bury. For the masses they kill, there is not enough ground perhaps in all of Amsterdam to bury the murdered. Burning is their answer.

When we were hiding in the Annexe, we would burn our refuse to get rid of any evidence of us being there.. We would burn our waste so as to reduce the danger to ourselves. Even then, the smoke from our chimney at different hours of the day (in summer particularly), exposed us for who we were and for what we were doing. I sometimes wonder in our discussions of how we were found, if maybe the smoke in the summer from our chimney was the culprit.

Now I see the smoke rising from this camp – morning, noon, and night. It is practical in the mind of the Nazis, and it is systematic. It is also a way to reduce the evidence of the mass atrocities they are committing should they lose the war and the truth be discovered. Yet, even as they burn the bodies to hide the evidence, surely the Allies see the smoke. Surely, they know as it is not coming from an industrial plant, that the Nazis are killing and burning human beings caught in their web of hatred.

Friday, October 20, 1944

Kitty,

"Margot's gone!"

We are to have no visitors in our scabies barrack, but somehow Mother got by the guards. She ran in greatly afraid and alarmed. She said, "In the middle of the night, they came into our barracks and turned the lights on in ours and the ones across from us. They called out numbers, "A-25239". I let out a loud sigh of shock, but quickly covered my mouth when the guard glared at me. They called the number again, "A-25239". That is Margot's number. Mother said, "I grabbed her arm, holding her in place. The guard said, 'If I call this number one more time, there will be more going. And you know what I mean!' Margot bravely got out of bed, walked past our castles of wooden planks, and joined the other girls at the door. I began to cry." At this news, I began to cry too from my sickbed. Mother said, "We could not sleep the rest of the night. The other ladies were as shocked and certain of the outcome. Anne, are there only two of us left?"

Is there only one loved one of mine left? "Please God don't let it be so. Please God, let her be alright. Bring her back to us, please. That is our prayer."

Mother was ordered out of my barrack. It was clear that people around me had heard our conversation and were growing troubled. We all fear our barrack slides right into the gas chamber where it sits. I did not want her to go. I lay in my bed the rest of the day; the itching wasn't as bad because my worries were far worse. Father. Now, Margot? Please no.

Saturday, October 21, 1944

Dearest Kitty,

How do they expect Mother to work today? How can any of us trapped here go out and live like nothing is wrong. We're to carry stones, dig potatoes, clean latrines, sew garments of prisoners-now-gone, and act like we never had a husband or father, like we never had a daughter or a sister. Others have faced this before we got here, and since we have arrived. I think this is why we see faces now absent of all emotion. Their eyes are blank. They have shut-off the side of themselves that once cared, remembered, and loved. That's what it looks like from inside here. Surely not.

It's one thing to be shut up here, locked in worry. It's another thing entirely to have to work and function outside, doing work that is nonsensical, while perhaps the smoke that now appears on the horizon is her daughter, my sister. I don't know how Mother is going to cope. I hope she comes by this evening. If not, am I all that is left?

Sunday, October 22, 1944

Dearest Kitty,

I have been reunited again. Margot joined me here. She's not real appreciative now that she sees what they have done to this place. Where has she been? Who cares! But I won't leave you hanging. When they rounded up the girls with Margot, some of the commanders were rotating out and others were rotating in, very quickly. They needed some strong girls to clean up the SS living quarters so that the new batch of tyrants would have a nice place to stay.

Margot regaled me with stories of how the other half lives in this community, beyond the wire. She said those soldiers have beautiful, cute houses with window boxes, gardens in the back, and ample food in the cellar. She also says that the houses she cleaned once belonged to Jewish families. She knew that by the mezuzahs on their doorposts. It is interesting that many of the finest homes in this area belonged to hard-working, Jewish families. Truly, God's Favor had once been on His people. We wondered what happened to those families. Did their lives follow the path to this place and up?

What really got me boiling mad was when Margot told me about seeing one of the young officers and his family. He was blond-headed, slender, with a kind face walking with his wife and two children – a son and a daughter. She believed both were under the age of eight. Margot was amazed how loving he was. He watched after them, carried his son across the street, while holding the hand of his daughter as he looked both ways, then crossed over safely. He kissed his wife and kids, and then headed to the office at Auschwitz where he would oversee the wholesale slaughter of our children, our mothers, and our fathers. How dare he! Do they not see the disconnect? Do they not see that we care for our kids the same? Does he not think we deserve to be back in our homes, and safe on our streets? I do not say curse words because Pim taught us not to, but if I did!

I am going to change the subject, Kit. Mother is hustling to get double portions of food to us. We are so happy to be the three of us again. I held really tight to Margot when she arrived. Mother ran in and kissed us both all over. Once again, Mother was able to get past the guard to see us after she heard from a friend that Margot was last seen being escorted here. How funny it is that Margot went from Barrack 29 to some SS officers' future homes, and then straight to the scabies barrack. While cleaning an officer's home, a doctor came by to check on the officer, saw Margot, and immediately sent her out and to here. She said that the officer looked sick to his stomach thinking that he or his precious family may have been exposed to scabies. I bet they sterilize that whole house or burn it down knowing a scabies-infested Jew had infiltrated their sacred barrier.

Anyway, Mother is bartering all kinds of things to get us food. She reminds me of the woman that the Bible describes in Proverbs 31. I cannot remember much of that chapter, except for the resourcefulness of the woman. In that passage, God's Word says something like, "The woman's husband trusts her. The children are clothed by her. Her household is neat and clean. She sews, plants, sells, and cuts deals to feed her family." Is this not our Mother?

I talked to Margot about Mother and this chapter in the Bible. Margot helped me remember it. The one thing I remembered about the text was there was no mention of love or affection in any of those verses. Then it hit me. This was a great description of our mother. She had never been good at loving on us or listening to our hearts. All she knew was to provide, to meet our needs, and to sacrifice for our wants. Mother was loving us the way she knew how to love us. How good is that?

I think of Mrs. Van Daan. She told Peter all the time how much she loved him, but her complaining and selfishness never matched her words. Mother never really loved us with words, but she showed it with her deeds. Oh, how I have misjudged her. If I get the chance, I hope to let her know that I am sorry for not understanding. If I do not get the chance, will you tell her?

Yours, Anne M. Frank

Monday, October 23, 1944

Dearest Kitty,

I had a fun conversation with Margot today while we lay on this hard, cold, damp floor incubating more scabies babies. It is terrible we are both here and at the same time wonderful. Here's what I mean:

Me: "I heard your sigh"

Margot: "I didn't sigh"

Me: "Yes, you did. You always sigh when you think you've messed up."

Margot: "I do not!"

Me: "Oh yes, you do, big sister. I bet you're regretting missing that transport, aren't you?"

Margot laughs: "That wasn't a sigh, but come to think of it...."

Me: "That's what I thought. You are just like Father. You do and do for others and never complain, but the sigh tells the whole story."

Margot: "I completely forgot about that attribute of Pim. Do you really think I am like him?"

Me: "Yes. You are Pim in a dress – a blue-striped prison dress I might add."

Margot: "You must be hallucinating. Are you okay? They took all our clothes when we got in here. I know I am skinny, but surely you can tell when I have nothing on!?

Me: "I have been here too long. I don't even notice naked anymore."

Margot: "I have been here so long, I cannot tell who is sick and who is well. We all kind of look the same."

Me; "I am sorry that you and Mother missed the transport. If you would have taken it, you may have still gotten the scabies, but you would have a chance to..."

Margot: "Sister, we are in this together. From a human standpoint, we are all we have. Remember, Father and Mother always told us their longing was for us to be close our whole lives, to live in the same town, to live near each other, to spend time together, to continue the legacy of our family."

Me: "I know, but still. What legacy can we leave if we all..."

Margot: "Don't say that, Anne. You are the one with the pluck and determination. You may see me as the big sister, but I see you as our strength. As long as you can face it, I know I can. You challenge me with your resolve. When I would pull into my shell, Mother would point to you and tell me that we should be as confident and sure as Anne. She said you were a dreamer who was not content to just dream, but to fulfill those dreams. She told me to swallow hard and keep pushing like you."

Anne; "I can't believe that. Mother always told me I should be obedient and kind and quiet like you."

Margot: "I guess she thought she saw the good points in both of us and tried to overlap them."

Anne: "I am glad you stayed. I am so glad you are here."

Margot; "Me too. Now let's get out of here quickly!"

Anne: "Agreed."

What a wonderful thing that God gave us when He gave us family. I have said before that God has never left me. Even in the worst situation, He shows me goodness. I am not alone. He is with me and so is my mother and sister. We have not been led to the end of the camp. At least the three of us (and four if you count Mrs. Van D) are all here and accounted for, waiting and hoping.

Yours, Anne M Frank

Tuesday, October 24, 1944

Dearest Kitty,

We received the double portion of bread today from under the hole by way of Mother. A sad note came with it that makes us worry so. It told us that Mother is not eating, that she is frantic for food, gathering it like a squirrel for winter, and finding it like a summer of drought. She walks the camp, searching, begging, and pleading for us, her daughters. The note said she doesn't sleep without finally giving in to exhaustion, saying our names over and over separated only with the prayer, "God please help them."

The sweet lady who passed the note is encouraging us to get out as soon as they will let us because she fears Mother will lose her mind and life, perhaps in that order. If only she would get the scabies! We could be together. We would be hungry, but we would hunger together. I never realized how much her life depended on our lives. Margot says she knew that long ago, which is why Margot tried to stay near her apron.

I look at my rash and long for it to go, or for at least one of ours to go away. Nothing is happening. Why isn't anything happening? And the smoke blows in.

Yours, Anne M. Frank

Wednesday, October 25, 1944

Dearest Kitty,

It would be easy to go insane in solitude or isolation. This is what our barrack is like for the skin-inflamed. Thankfully, I have Margot to talk to, but today she got worried about me. She heard me talking to you!

I had to calm her down and convince her after giving her many proofs that I was still in my right mind. I let her know that I was keeping my diary still, but orally. She thought that was the craziest thing she had ever heard. She knew I kept my diary. The whole Annexe made fun of me for being so private with you. I had shared parts of it with Margot back in our room. She remembered that, but had no idea that I was still keeping one. I let her know that if and when we get out of this, I want to be a journalist and a writer. I told her the first thing I was going to write was "The Secret Annexe." After this became a hit on the bookstands, I was going to write a second book, "The Open Atrocities," as a sequel to describe our torment in this death camp.

Margot still did not understand. I told her, "When I am alone, Kitty helps me cope. Besides, I once read that if we state something verbally, even in a silent whisper, that the mind is better at remembering it later in life." I don't know if that is right Kitty, but it was a more convincing answer to keep Margot from having me moved to a mental barrack!

Still Yours, Anne M. Frank

Thursday, October 26, 1944

Dearest Kitty,

I guess we have reached the point of "too much of a good thing." Margot is acting as if I am getting on her nerves. I am not sure what her problem is, because honestly, it can't be my fault. I sure miss my books. How I longed for the day each week when Miep would bring us new books to read. This kept us from going stir-crazy, and it kept us from killing each other in that attic. The books opened my mind to other people, and transported me to new places. I don't like that word "transport." I hope to remove it from all my writing once my two books have been written.

I wish Pim would have gotten me that New Testament he had been working to get for me. I would love to learn more about Jesus and all He faced in His dear life as a Jewish teacher. I can imagine that I would find lots of coping skills from Him. I envy those who have Bibles in their homes and who study them every day and week. It is so sad how we take the things most valuable for granted. We don't appreciate much until it is taken away.

At first, we had heard it was just the Jews who the Nazis were wanting to exterminate. Then we heard it was the sick, the ill, and the retarded. Later, we realized that Christians joined the hunted list. I am seeing a stark difference in some of the Christians here, as opposed to the others. I had not thought about it much until Margot quit talking to me, so I let my mind stroll down another meandering corridor of thought. It seems Christians are more willing to die than the rest of us. We heard about a priest named Father Kolbe who had found himself here in Auschwitz.

When someone tries to escape this place or if they are successful in some rare and miraculous way, all others are punished. It was just like on the trains coming here. We were told if anyone escaped, the family in the train car and others would suffer death. Anyway, I think it is said, some people escaped, and the SS commandant ordered that ten other prisoners be thrown in the basement and starved to death. One of the ten chosen began to cry about his family, pleading for mercy. It was then that Father Kolbe asked if he could take the man's place. Believe it or not, the commandant let him. Nine of them starved to death, and Father Kolbe was left. They gave him an injection of poison to kill him. How amazing.

I just find it hard that anyone would be willing to die for someone else unless there is a life after this one. A woman in this infirmary was telling me how her husband had been killed here a few years back. Someone had smuggled a letter to her from him. She was later captured from her hiding place and now faces the same struggle we do. What I love about her is her faith in God and her faith in Jesus. She said her husband's letter spoke of seeing her one day soon in Heaven and how wonderful it will be to be together again, and forever. She said the Apostle Paul said that he and his fellow Christians faced death daily. I don't know what all he faced, but we can relate. We are facing death daily, which causes us to work in our hearts and minds to deal with the inevitable outcome of the Nazi plan.

Yours, Anne M. Frank

Friday, October 27, 1944

Dearest Kitty,

I don't want to bring you down with all this talk of death in my mental letters to you. I know you understand as you reason through the emotions I am feeling. As I said yesterday in my meanderings, we face death daily. It is here we realize it. But then, I wonder if you realize it too? How many people where you are realize that death is at the end of every life sentence?

Remember when I had that dream of Hanneli back when we were in exile? I saw her suffering in rags, crying for help. I prayed for God to bring her back to us. I prayed that God would let her live to the end of the war. And then the thought came to me; does Hanneli know God well enough to pray to Him for herself? I had never really considered this before. Did she know God or just know the rituals that people follow for a religion? I truly believe that I have a relationship with God. I pray to Him nightly, both when I was younger with my parents, and now all by myself. I prayed at first because my parents told me to. Now, I pray because I want to. I know Him. I really believe that. Does Hanneli know Him? It came to me then and even more now that people need to know God. There is no way to face what we face without Him and to come out unscarred or unmarred. I felt that even more as we were saying the Lord's Prayer in the barrack, and now only me here every Sunday.

People need to know God not just for this life. They desperately need to know God for the life to come. There is an eternal life far better than the most fantastic beauty this earth has to offer. There is an eternal death far worse than anything the Nazis can manufacture. How can I love people, care for people, even talk to people and take no concern for their souls? In my dream of Hanneli, my greatest regret was not that I could not help her in her state of torment, but that I had not told her about the love and care of the Living God.

I am praying, as soon as I close this letter to you Kitty, that I will be able to tell others about God. I want to care enough about Him and them, that I will at least ask. Maybe I will even begin with this supposed nurse who comes by to check on us. She comes not because she wants to, but because she is ordered to. We may all be prisoners here in some way. I believe firmly that this nurse could use God too.

Yours, Anne M. Frank

Saturday, October 28, 1944

My dearest Kitty,

Speaking of God, we need Him now! I mean right now! They have rousted us all off the floor. They have said don't bring anything. Dear God! This can mean only one thing. They are tired of us taking up space. We are headed to the chimney. Oh God, help us! Give us mercy or give us grace to face these next steps.

BERGEN-BELSEN

Sunday, October 29, 1944

Dearest Kitty,

We have been on a train now for a few hours. It is a terribly sad thing and we do not understand it. We are headed out of Auschwitz. That is good I think. But Mother is nowhere to be found. Where are we going? What will she do? What will we do without her? We haven't had Father since we were separated in the first selection. I pray somehow Pim is still alive. Even if I can't live, I want Pim to live. He is so dear and so good. We should be glad that we are leaving Auschwitz, but how can we leave this living Hell and be happy knowing that Mother and perhaps Father are still trapped there? How will Mother live without us? Will she continue to do without? Will she continue to murmur our names until she sleeps? Or, will she be able to trust in the God we prayed to, trusting us to His Care. We are trusting Him. We have no other option.

Margot is crying and holding on to me. I want to cry, but how can I? She said she trusts me to be strong. So, Kitty, I cry silently. You can know my heartache and fear. You're the only one I can share it with other than God. He is with us even in this train. I feel Him.

Yours, Anne M. Frank

Monday, October 30, 1944

Kitty,

It is so cold. We are poorly clothed. The only consolations in this cattle car are that Margot and I are together. There are so many people in here that warmth is achievable. We have clutched in our hands our only sustenance – a thick slice of bread, a cut of butter, and a piece of cheese. It is not much and we have no idea when we will get more, so we nurse it. They gave us a little water but it is gone. The place stinks as much as any latrine in Auschwitz. The only difference is, we could step around the excrement to a degree in camp. Here, we lie in it, as there is no other option.

We keep thinking that we can stand this, if when the train car doors open, we will be free. That is our hope. But if that is our longing, why do people in here act so hatefully. I do picture Hell where thousands upon thousands in misery are climbing on top of each other, trying to get out of the fire. Children are trampled, as are the women and the weak. Is this how people are to act? As broken as we are, we realize we either stand and push back or fall to be trampled debris on the floor. Margot and I have decided to stand. The last time in this mess, Pim guarded us. We just hid behind his protective shield. Now, we are thrust to do the same without him. At the early or late death of parents, I suppose every son or daughter has to realize that it is now up to him or her to stand on their own. We grasp that, but I am fifteen years-old. Margot is just eighteen years-old. We don't feel we are ready for this, but then I guess life doesn't care. We are ready when we are forced to make ready.

How much longer will this train ride last? We are exhausted. We are nauseated. The train slows. I won't bid you goodnight yet, Kitty. Are we there?

We are not. They just opened the doors for a minute, removed the dead, let us walk around for a minute in front of guns with the hammers pulled back, ready to fire. Would it be so terrible to be gunned down and let this misery end? It would be unless freedom is at the next stop. I don't want to quit one kilometer before freedom. How tragic would that be? What would Margot, Mother, or even Father say if they are gathered together in freedom and I had given up an hour too soon? They gave us some water after they saw the dead. We are back in the car, doors bolted, with a guard on the top. He is alert and ready to fire, though he shivers from the cold as the lone watchman. What must he think of his Fuhrer?

Yours, Anne M. Frank

Tuesday, October 31, 1944

Kitty,

We are under gunfire. The train has stopped. We heard guards scream, "Take cover!."

We hear the sound of running on the roof and the pounding of bombs. The guards flee for their safety and leave us here for the doom that was meant for them. Can someone tell the Allies that we are the victims? We are not German troops heading to the front. We are Jewish prisoners being led, we suppose, to safer confines for the Germans or to freedom for us. Make them stop! I remember the bombs in Amsterdam. I hated the sound. Then, I was so afraid that I would run up and down the attic stairs just to drown out the noise. I cannot even move an inch in here. I feel like a puppy tied to a table in a house that is burning down, and the family has fled in their fear – forgetting about me. My only hope of drowning out the bombs is the deafening cries of the children in here and the screams of the men and women.

I even screamed, "Heaven help us! God, please tell them we are here! Kill our captors, but spare us please!"

It died down, Kitty. We are on the move again. I have no real idea if it is day or night. It is so dark from an approaching storm. I hear the thunder blended with the bombs. The clouds are thick. The rain is heavy. It may be midnight or it may be midday. It is hard to update you per our normal schedule because we have no idea. I just hope God sends the hail as large as millstones. We are in the safety of an armored prison wagon. May our captors be knocked out, but only after they unlock our doors.

Wednesday, November 1, 1944

Dearest Kitty,

I am laying in a tent at a place called Bergen-Belsen. This is not where I thought we were going to end up. I had better hopes a few hours ago. The storm still pounds and the winds are whipping feverishly. What we wouldn't give for a sturdy structure to rest in. What happened to us? How did we get here?

Let me tell you the story. There was a pause in the storm and the skies lit up. There were heavy clouds, but the sun illuminated them. When the doors slid open with that rolling screech, we had to squint our eyes walking from our darkness into the light. Kitty, what an amazing sight! There were trees and grass. We had been released into a forest. The smells were exhilarating. All of the stench just wafted away from our noses with a welcomed cleansing. It seems that Hellish ride was behind us. The guards were still before us – and behind us – and surrounding us.

Our limbs were tight and our bodies cold. Again, if this is the tunnel to freedom, we can bear it. They gathered us in a loose formation and we began to march. Margot pointed out some people we knew as she scanned the group, with a hope we would see Mother. Rachel was there as was Jenny. Jenny had once been in our barrack with us in Auschwitz. We passed through a town on the way. It was beautiful. How I hoped this would be our town. Maybe this is where they would settle us for the duration of the war. That is what I hoped. I could see Margot and me here. It just felt like a place where we could easily belong, a place that I had envisioned moving to when I got married and had children with Peter or with the other Peter. I was so disappointed when we walked through it without stopping. Some nice people there did hand out some blankets to those who would look them in the face. I looked, and a kind old lady pitched me a blanket as the guards looked away. I saw a few others doing the same. Margot and I wrapped it around us. It was small, but it helped. It was clean, fresh, and warm. It was ours.

We reached the camp, but there was no room for us. Quickly the guards with some other prisoners put up tents. The rain began to pour again, and our blanket was getting soaked. We shivered and watched, and hoped. Finally, as each tent was finished, many ran in to flee the wet and the freezing cold. Margot and I kept getting pushed back. I would lunge forward. She would drag back. The blanket became her leash on me, her wayward pet. I finally gave her a sharp word that we needed shelter, "Let's go." We were the last to enter our tent.

The ground inside this tent is sopping wet. It is still cold, but thankfully we are covered. I just pray this tent can hold up in this wind. Why is everything so hard?

Thursday, November 2, 1944

Dearest Kitty,

The tent is barely standing. It collapsed near daybreak, and the rain was forced in by the monsoon. You would think they would have repaired the tent for us, but why would the Germans do that? I heard one of them say "You dogs should be grateful!" Dogs? That is a terrible term to a Jewish mind. Dogs? That is how they saw us. Not the dogs that you take home and care for, but the ravaging, stray dogs that you shoot out of fear they will hurt your chickens or your children. Dogs? That explains a lot to me.

We are given numbers and treated as firewood. Now we are given common nouns describing us as flea-bitten animals: dogs. That term fits in another way. They eat the food and give us the scraps. They bite into a piece of meat to find that the mouthful is fat and bone. They spit it out, but don't want to waste it. They throw what they spat out to us and expect us to wag our tails and be grateful. Is this better than Auschwitz? I see no smoke from a burning furnace. Perhaps.

Friday, November 3, 1944

Dearest Kitty,

They moved us into a wooden barrack. We were the last to be assigned to this one. Needless to say, we are stuck by the door. You would think this would be great, but when you are trying to stay warm and dry, this is the worst place to be. Oh well, it could be worse. We could be in the smoke ascending.

We still have a mild case of scabies, but that doesn't seem to bother anyone here. It seems the sick and the well are housed together. Compared to the scabies barrack, this place is a luxury apartment. We are sleeping two or three to a bed, and it is a bunk with straw which is far better than the cold concrete.

I don't know what tomorrow holds for us, but what's new? We are never told what the next day will be. We are like pieces of furniture moved and not consulted. It seems the war is far away at the moment, as is our Mother and Father.

Speaking of Father – if Father was killed when we arrived in Auschwitz, which I fear he was, there was no funeral service for him, no eulogy given, nor a newspaper obituary for such a fine man. If we were back at home in Holland and Pim had died, Margot and I would be doing most of the funeral planning. She and Mother would choose the casket and bring the handsome suit he always wore for special occasions. While they did that, I would be the one writing the obituary – quite naturally. Each must do what their talents direct. I am thinking, what would I say about my father, Otto Frank? What do I want the rest of the world to know? I think I would have written the obituary this way. Please take note, Kitty, because I do not have a pen and paper handy.

Otto Heinrich Frank was born in Frankfurt Germany to Michael and Betty Frank on May 12, 1889. After graduating from high school, he attended the University of Frankfurt for a short while, studying history. Seeing his father's need, Mr. Frank worked at the family bank for a year while taking courses in economics to better assist in the family business. He later worked a year in New York for Macy's department store and for a bank in that area.

He returned to Germany to help with the family banking business. When World War I began, Otto Frank served valiantly for his homeland, being promoted to the rank of lieutenant. He was recognized early in life as a leader of men. After the war, his family lost much of their business and assets. Mr. Frank refused to look back. On his 36th birthday, May 12, 1925, he gave himself the best gift yet – a wife named Edith Hollander. They were married twenty years.

With a wife and a baby on the way, Mr. Frank went out on his own to start the Opecta Company, which experienced notable success. From that venture, he began a second company called Pectacon. Mr. Frank provided work for many hard-working men and women and gave them benefits unseen in his industry. He saw every person working for him as a friend, not as a hired hand. He cared about these families and was very lenient and generous in their times of need. Often when business was slow, he would cut his own pay to keep all his employees working without ever reducing their wages or hours.

On February 16, 1926, Mr. Frank added another title to his name, "Father." Mrs. Frank gave birth to a beautiful, healthy baby girl whom they named Margot Betti Frank. How thrilled he was to be a father of a little girl. Growing up with two brothers and not having a sister until later, he had dreamed of having a girl all his own. That was good, because three years later, on June 12, 1929, Edith and Otto greeted another sweet gift, Annelies Marie Frank. What a happy family they made. Mr. Frank was an amazing father, praying with them at night, comforting them when they hurt, taking interest in their passions, and being a listening ear when they longed to be heard.

In 1933, Germany became less and less safe for Jewish families. Otto Frank took the initiative to start a branch of his company in Amsterdam and moved his family there out of harm's way. Mr. Frank always had great instincts and anticipation, which helped him in business and in life. When the Germans invaded Holland, pressure was once again placed on Jewish families. In his warehouse on 263 Prinsengracht, Otto Frank set up a hiding place for his family to retreat to should the need arise. The need did.

He had planned everything down to the last detail – another talent of Mr. Frank. He even provided safe haven for four others. Because his fellow workers loved their boss Mr. Frank so much, they risked their lives to keep the entire Frank family and their friends safe in the hiding place for over two years. This was quite an amazing feat at that time. Why would they do that? They knew that Mr. Frank would do the same for them, and that he had done so much for them in their lives already.

It was Mr. Frank's foresight that spared his family, even though they would ultimately be arrested, imprisoned at Westerbork, and eventually at Auschwitz. Otto Frank died on September 5, 1944, at the hands of the Nazis in the Auschwitz Death Camp in Poland. He protected his family and employees who hid him to the very end.

Mr. Frank is preceded in death by his father Michael Frank. He is survived by his mother Betty Frank, his loving wife Edith Frank, two beautiful daughters whom he loved dearly, Margot and Anne Frank. He is also survived by his brother Robert Frank, brother Herbert Frank, and sister Helene Frank. He will be dearly missed as a son, a brother, a husband, a father, a business partner, generous employer, and dear friend. What we will treasure most is his love, his zeal for life, his gregarious personality, and the way he lit up every room he entered.

Hold on to this obituary, Kitty. I am hoping it is not needed. I wonder who will write my obituary one day? I pray it is not needed either for a long, long time.

Yours, Anne M. Frank

Saturday, November 4, 1944

My dearest Kitty,

Today was a great day for us. We are around a lot of Dutch Jews, many who know us or knew our parents. I think I am the youngest here in our bunk area. The SS aren't sure what they want to do with us. Unlike the Nazi way, there is no organization as of yet. We have been able to wander a little more freely here. We have access to a little water. We are able to clean ourselves and there is food given to us at the wire by people who wander up. We have nurses around us. They are fellow-prisoners, but they can at least care for some of our hurts and sicknesses.

Down from our barracks, there is a barrack of children. They all seem to be from Holland. They have no parents with them, and they are very young. They look afraid and lonely. It's like finding a child on your front door. You look around and can't see who left the little one, so you take them in. That is what we have been able to do. Margot and I went down to where we heard the children were and played with them. How great was that! The children have no idea what they are facing. They just long for mummy or father. They have no concept of war and peace. For the most of them, this is all they have ever known. It is not war or peace; it is just life.

When playing with these children, I feel my life matters. Margot and I feel we have purpose. We are not hauling rocks, or moving sod, nor are we breaking down batteries for no evident purpose. We are caring for children. This is what I want to do in my writing. God has given me the ability to write, but not for glory or for selfish gain. These things may come, but the real drive is to use my gifts to help people. I especially want to help children. Few can see through their eyes, but I can. If we make it out of here, you will see!

Yours, Anne M. Frank

Sunday, November 5, 1944

My dearest Kitty,

I want you to know that Margot would make a wonderful mother. She is so intelligent and comprehending. She seems to know what works best to soothe each child. It is amazing to watch her. She takes one tact with this child and another with that one. Each child is different as night and day; yet Margot knows the combination to unlock each one. I am not that way, at least not yet. But, what a joy!

No sooner do I see the joy, then I see the harsh reality of death everywhere. Death was somewhat hidden in our last camp. People were there and then they were gone. We saw corpses on the ground, but they were quickly carried away and burned. Here, just from the short time we have been here, I see people who have been dead not just for a day or two, but in all manner of decay appearing to have been so for a very long time. As terrible as this is, when we see these children and we are able to hug them and listen to them, the heartache here just melts away. Is this what God feels like when He looks on and loves fallen humanity?

Margot and I have discussed this at length today. As we were about to close down for the night, she whispered to me, "Let's say that prayer." I agreed whole-heartedly. We prayed it aloud, hoping someone would join in. There are many here from different languages still, though our majority seems to be Dutch. We prayed "Our Father which art in

Heaven." We hoped people would pick up on it, but someone yelled, "Be quiet!" So, we finished it in a whisper, just Margot and me.

Yours, Anne M. Frank

Monday, November 6, 1944

My dearest Kitty,

Still not much to do today. We are so glad. We were with the children again. A little boy named Hans has really taken a liking to me. He is with me everywhere I go. He draws pictures for me at night. He gives me kisses on the cheek. He smiles and hugs my leg while I try to walk. He loves to stand on my feet facing me, so that while I walk, he is walking backwards, laughing (I remember doing the same at his age when Father would come home). Before long, all the other children want to take their turn. Margot and some of the other ladies join in the fun.

One of my favorite times is when I tell the kids, "It is story-time!" They all gather around me, sit on the floor, legs folded, arms together, hands in a prayer position, with chins resting on their hands. I had been writing stories when we were in the Annexe. I have tried some of the lighter ones on these children. They seem to really enjoy them. Margot even seems impressed. Other times, I will tell them of Greek mythology which I have loved to read, but render the stories different as human actors so as to not confuse the children into some sort of polytheism.

I could just tell stories all day. We are all hungry. We are all infested. It is as if a dust follows us everywhere we go. I am not sure if that dust is dirt or death, but we each see it as we walk and come upon each other. But, these children? If they can feel love here. If they can make it out of here. Maybe, they will grow up to stop hatred and war. If my influence can help move them in that way, I could die right here and know my life has mattered. I can know that Anne Frank has served a greater purpose.

Yours, Anne M. Frank

Tuesday, November 7, 1944

Dearest Kitty,

Back in the barracks, things aren't as sweet. It is when we are here that we feel the cold. Why is it that we feel the oneness of humanity in the children's barrack, and retreat to the haven of selfishness when we return? Is it that in our barrack we taste the reality of our existence? I don't want to remove myself from caring. I want us to love each other as we love those kids. Aren't we all children anyway? I know we act like it. If we could become more like those kids, happy with a smile and a hug, what a better place this place would be.

Kit, are you ever in a bad mood? I don't remember you ever snapping at me. Pim never did. I hurt him a few times, especially when I wrote that letter telling him in essence that I didn't need him. He was hurt but never hurtful. I want that in me. I want this sword to become a plowshare. I want this for our whole world.

Yours, Anne M. Frank

Wednesday, November 8, 1944

Dearest Kitty,

Alas, organization has come to Belsen. They called us out for roll call. Back to our numbers. A-25237 and A-25239. We were ordered to attention in our familiar fives. Our five were assigned to the out-door trash pick-up. How we wanted to be in the potato detail or the cleaning detail. In the potato detail, we could maybe eat something extra. In the cleaning detail, we could be inside and warm. But because we still had traces of scabies, outside we did go. We have no coats, no pants, and no head-covers. It was as if we were cast into the cold to do what good we could before we fell to the bitter elements. Then, we would become the trash to be picked-up and discarded.

While picking up trash, we came upon a horrific smell. We saw a mound of dirt with birds flying in and out. As we got closer, the smell grew worse. We were hesitant to go there; in fact, we did not want to go there but the Kapo ordered us to. Why? Because, he thought he saw a piece of trash there on the edge of that mound. We drew closer and quickly realized the white piece of trash was not a piece of paper. It was the sleeve of a skeleton, whose arm was draped over the mound. I threw up what little I had in my stomach; more of a dry heave than anything. The guard laughed. He said, "Take a long look. You will get to know these residents real soon." I was horrified. Margot passed out.

The guard kicked her and yelled, "Oh no. Not yet. It's not your time. There is still trash to pick up!" and he kicked her again. She opened her eyes, and I wrapped her arm around my shoulder, guiding her up. I lifted the sleeve of the deceased arm and pushed it back into the pit. We then quickly moved on with our duties. There was no erasing that scene. In that pit, there are thousands upon thousands of the dead. Why an open pit? Well, to gather more in. All of a sudden, the burning fires of Birkenau seemed merciful and humane. Surely up in smoke is better than this.

Yours, Anne Frank

Thursday, November 9, 1944

Dearest Kitty,

Margot and I didn't get to visit last night when we got in. She was disturbed and I was too. We did not speak of what we had seen to others or to each other. You are the only one I have told. We did our trash pick-up on the other side of camp and were able to stray near the children's barrack. Hans saw me, but at first didn't recognize me. As I passed, I gave him a wink and he ran toward me calling, "Miss Anne! Miss Anne! Come tell us a story!? Before he could reach me, the guard shoved him back, but not too hard. He spoke sternly, but not meanly. To the child, he voiced as a father, not a killer. Hans returned with a whimper and I continued on with a tear.

On this side of camp there is life. On the other side of camp, there is death. From what we had seen, I told Margot my wishes when I die. "Let me be buried quickly in the Jewish fashion or let me be..." I swallowed hard, "Let me be cremated. I do not want my body to be allowed to decay for all to see." Margot agreed and reminded me of an amazing verse from her study of the Old Testament. She could not remember the exact place, but said somewhere in the Book of Psalms, King David said, "You will not let Your Holy One see decay." "That's what I want, my sister" I said. "I do not want my body to see decay, not like that." She said the same.

Yours, Anne M. Frank

Friday, November 10, 1944

Dearest Kitty,

If you were to ask, "How is the food? You have said nothing about the food.." I would have to tell you the reason I don't talk about food is because there is so little. We are literally starving to death here. My stomach has shrunk, yet it extends out in a pooch. I get full with the tiniest of bites, which they give us sometimes every third day. We go to the fence, hoping for someone, anyone to give us something to eat. The guards threaten us and the few people outside the fences who are there hoping to see a missing loved one. It is as if the guards are saying to the outsiders, "Don't feed the animals!"

We don't speak of food because even the talk makes us long for what we know we cannot have. I have dreams nearly every night of sitting at the table with Mother and Father. The dishes are passed around. We all get what we want and then there is much left over. We are all full, but there are leftovers put away. What would that be like? I can hardly remember. I have to forget.

Taken for granted. This is a common refrain in my thoughts. What I wouldn't give to step into a kitchen, grab a spoon, and ladle out some of Mother's great cooking onto my plate. We have no kitchen connected to where we live.

Taken for granted. I never realized what a luxury it was to walk into a toilet and close the door for privacy in doing my business. I think Dussel may have had it right with all those bathroom trips. He took advantage of the privilege while he had it. Even that being the case, all that is behind us. I long for privacy. I long for a modicum of decency and modesty.

Taken for granted. I never took for granted the chance to have a table to sit at and read and do my studies. I had to argue and fight for Dussel to give me just a few hours, a couple of days a week. He finally relented. I have no desk here to argue over. I have no books. I hated maths, but I would gladly take that up again, if only I could have a table and a chair.

Taken for granted. I hated sharing my room with Dussel with all his snoring and gasping for breath. It irritated me to no end to hear him up praying and rocking back and forth on his heels every Sunday morning while I was trying to sleep. All that seemed like such an inconvenience. Now I am housed with over 100 women, I guess, which is less than what we had in our Auschwitz chicken pen. I would love to be in a room with just me and one other person, even that dentist in the Annexe. I would trade all these ladies for Dussel any day. Margot was a better roommate growing up, and I complained about her too. Now I have her back, which is great, but we are joined by the masses of the sick, dying, and doomed.

Taken for granted. Life was. Each day was. It is depressing that we are counted in the numbers of the sick, dying, and doomed now. We have become the "nearly departed." If we are blessed to get out of here, I can say with the highest level of confidence, I will never take any of these things for granted again.

I am so hungry.

Yours, Anne M. Frank

Saturday, November 11, 1944

Dearest Kitty,

You know what they say, "There is good day, and there are bad days." I know that's not what they say, but it is pretty close, and it is true in this place. For every good day, there are many bad days. We had our roll call and then our work detail assignments. Margot and I were assigned the trash heap. Just as we got started, the "old ball and chain" guard had to run to the latrine. He came back for a while, then he ran back to the latrine. Finally, he told us to return to our barrack, "Schnell!" We did. He was gone for the day. I guess it was something he ate. I wish we would have been able to eat it in his place. I would gladly take the runs to the latrine (play on words) than to have nothing to take to the latrine.

What did we do with all our free time? You ought to know the answer; we scrounged for food. We went to the fence. There were always saddened people there who would call out names of family members, but then would be chased off by the guards. As much as they were threatened, they continued to return. Love has a way of doing that. When we love, we take all kinds of risks, and accept all sorts of inconveniences. Father did that when Margot's name was called for work duty in some far-away place. He chose hardship over safety. He risked his life to save hers and ours.

That is what I found fascinating about this sweet, old, wrinkled lady who continually came to our fence, day after day. She came calling the same name over and over, "Natasha, Natasha." The guards would come to where she was, point their guns toward her and tell her to leave. Once they even fired one into the air to scare her. Each time, she would leave with tears silently rolling down her cheeks, head down, walking slowly, and looking back every ten or twelve meters. We would think that was the last, but the next day she was there again. I think the guards got tired of messing with her and gave her some leeway, like my teacher did when he realized he could not keep me from talking. We were so hungry. We would often go to the fence and as they begged for a loved one, we begged for food. We didn't understand them well, and they didn't necessarily understand us, but they could say a name and we could rub our stomachs and put our hands to our mouths. They knew what we wanted and needed, and we knew who they needed and wanted.

This sweet old lady, our frequent visitor, came one day while we were picking up trash near the fence. Twice, I had to sit down because of my dizziness. She repeated the frequent name, "Natasha? Natasha?" We tried to make her understand that we would ask around for Natasha, though we knew no one by that name. Our complex was connected and divided by fences. We could call out names from one section to another. We tried to let her know we would do that. I then motioned to her, asking her if she had anything we could eat. We were so weak from not having eaten even a piece of bread in over four days. She signaled that she understood, and pointed to her watch. It was almost 12:00 noon. She then pointed at the 2:00 on her watch and gave us the impression she would be back with food. We have no watches. They took those away from us at the Annexe. If we would have had some, we would have pawned them for bread by now. So, we just hovered around the fence as if there was a whole lot of trash there. In fact, we would pick up a piece and drop two pieces when the guard wasn't looking. The wind helped us a lot because we could hold up a piece of litter and the wind would carry it toward the fence. We were too weak to stay upright, but the thought of food gave us a renewed strength and energy, and made us willing to brave the cold and the shaky legs a little while longer.

It paid off. She came back with a quarter of a loaf of bread. We could not openly take it while the guards watched, so I went to ask the guard a question, while Margot got the bread and slid it under her ragged garb. We then went back to the barrack. Most were still out working. We gave thanks, real thanks, and we ate as if it was a wedding feast, or a funeral repast. It wasn't near what we needed, but it was something.

We did look for Natasha because we knew that this sweet lady would be at the fence the next day, and we did not want to disappoint her or avoid her. Sadly, no Natasha could be found. The woman continued to come a few days more. It made it so awkward for us. We felt we had betrayed her and used her. Finally, she quit coming, but I don't think she quit looking. I believe she probably checked every transport as they walked through their little town.

Yours, Anne M. Frank

Sunday, November 12, 1944

Dearest Kitty,

And then there are more bad days. It was extremely cold last night. We are not even into December yet. We lost two ladies in our barrack. One woman laid head-to-head to me. We roused at the call, but she just lay there. I, at first, was jealous and hated to wake her. No one sleeps that soundly in this place. When you get to, you surely want to enjoy it to the fullest. I touched her. She was cold. Cold does not mean death here. We are all cold to the touch it seems. Our cheeks are cold. Our hands are cold. Our feet are definitely cold. I shook her, "Andi wake-up." It was then I realized she was lifeless. Her body lay there, but it was absent of life. How sad. I was bothered by this. I looked at my hand and could not believe what it had touched.

That "what" is a problem too. The word cadaver or corpse is such an inanimate noun. It describes something, not someone. I think this is what the SS troops see in us, something, not someone. This is why I believe they shave our heads and tattoo our arms. They do not call out our names, but our numbers. The "Who am I" game from back at Auschwitz comes to my mind. I repeat it to myself, "I am Annelies Marie Frank. I am a fifteen-year-old writer, the youngest daughter of Otto and Edith Frank, sister of Margot. I was born in Frankfurt Germany on June 12, 1929, and moved to Holland at a young age. I am the future wife of somebody, maybe a guy named Peter. I will be the mother of three children.

We will have a home all our own. Many books will line our living room – many I have written, and more I have read."

They ordered us out. Then some of our inmates/roommates were assigned to discard the dead. I am so glad that is not our job. They pull them out of each barrack and lay them on the ground ever so irreverently, like stacks of wood. All day long, we step over these people, not corpses. I want to look them in the face. I want to construct their story. I want the world to know who they are, where they were born, who their parents, siblings, and children are. I want to tell what they did for a living, where they went to school, what they liked to read, what they did that was memorable, and what they did that was so roaringly funny. Everyone deserves that.

I want them to have a grave with a headstone and some flowers. I want there to be a definitive, exact, confirmed place where they lay, so loved ones can come to that exact site, above that exact body, and pray. This is not too much to ask for anyone.

I have to keep moving. We have to keep moving, always moving. We must stay one step ahead of death. Margot and I are squeezed together in our bed after a hard day of clean-up. I really think the guards throw their trash out there on purpose, just to give us a job to do. We say our prayers as we lay under our one blanket that we have held onto since the moment we arrived.

Yours, Anne Frank

Monday, November 13, 1944

Dearest Kitty,

The guards are getting grumpy. I think they have heard bad news from the front. My question is why are they keeping us here? Why are they keeping us alive? What value do we have to them? We are doing nothing productive other than work in hopes for scant sustenance. They are working us, perhaps, just to keep us busy and worn down enough that we won't try to escape. What do they fear from us? If we're not busy, we will mutiny? We haven't the strength to get out of bed. Sometimes, we just lie in bed hoping to die. Would it have been better to be gassed the minute we arrived in Auschwitz? Perish the thought. As long as we are alive, there is hope.

Our bodies get out of the wooden slabs for morning roll call that lasts hours on end. Standing for roll call is worse than working. Our bodies march to orders and dutifully obey every growl. We do not look human. I try to avoid looking at myself. A woman I knew walked by. I asked, "How are you doing, Rootje?" She looked at me and said, "Fine, but excuse me. How do I know you?" I told her ashamedly, "I am Anne Frank." She looked me over from head to toe. She got close to my face and looked into my eyes. Then she said, "Oh Anne, please forgive me. My eyes aren't as good as they once were." I knew she was lying. Her eyes were fine, but my face was not. I have changed. I am a skeleton with a thin layer of flesh. I looked at Margot for the first time. I mean, I really looked at her. If I had not been with her all this time, I would not have known her. I have seen her waste away so gradually that her appearance is no shock to me. It's like seeing one of my favorite movie stars, whose pictures were plastered on my wall. I have pictures of them in their prime, at the peak of stardom in the old movies I once watched. Then later, to see their pictures in my Movie Star Gossip magazines, I am repulsed by how they have aged. They are not recognizable. I have to look really closely, and then compare that magazine picture to their photo on my wall. After a while, I see the same eyes, surrounded by a melting face. This is what they see in me.

We see the lifeless bodies hauled off in wheelbarrows pushed by the near-lifeless. We see skeletons pushing skeletons and it no longer shocks us. I am glad you are not seeing this Kitty. You see it through my eyes, which is the sanitized version of what is here.

Yours, Anne M. Frank

Tuesday, November 14, 1944

Dearest Kitty,

We have tried the "Who am I" game here with just a few ladies still strong enough to speak. It did not go as planned. There was no lift in the exercise. One lady, Wilma, told us:

"I am Wilma Lechler, the wife of Fredrick Lechler. He has no idea where I am. We had a fight this past August. The pressure was getting to both of us. The curfews forced us to stay together more than we had ever been together in our lives. Food was short. Fear was huge. His inconsiderate habits had been eating at me for weeks. Looking at the star on his shirt just made me even more angry. He wore his as a sign of pride, "I'm Jewish! I am not ashamed of that. I want all to know that I am Jewish. I like to be with Jewish people. I only want to do business with Jewish people. I think kids should go to Jewish schools so we don't lose our religion or our culture." He saw the good side, perhaps the cultural side of the star. I saw a target. I felt the looks of disdain. I felt them from the non-Jewish, and I felt them from those who hid that they were Jewish. I wanted to leave. Fredrick said this would pass.

I told him that I could not be with a man who would tolerate such Hitleresque practices. He said that maybe I married the wrong man. I told him that maybe I had. With that, I grabbed my coat and left. I wasn't really going to leave him. I had nowhere to go, especially in the allotted time we could be out. But I wanted to scare him. I wandered the streets for an hour and then started back, upset with myself that I had to head home. No sooner did I get to our street, then one of the Gestapo agents stopped me and asked for my ID. I showed it to him, still upset. He signaled to a truck. I could only see its front bumper and the steering wheel inside the front window, with the head of a man straining to look our way behind it. The lights came on. The truck started, turned the corner, and pulled up beside us. A uniformed man came out of the back with his gun pointed right at me. He told me to get in. I asked him, 'What have I done?' He said, 'You were born! Get in!'

They forced me into the truck and sped me away. That was the last I saw of Fredrick. Poor Fredrick. What have I done to him? I love him. I would never really leave him. I remember our courtship, our walks in the moonlight, the poems he would write me, and the plans we had made. Poor, poor Fredrick. What does he think now? That I didn't love him? That I left him? Or, does he realize I was picked up and shipped out to a camp? How it must have hurt when I didn't come home. If I knew this would have happened, I would have avoided the argument. I would have let him know that I loved him. If we had to be separated, at least he would be consoled by the knowledge that his wife would die for him. What must he be thinking if he still is alive? Whether he is home, in hiding, or in a camp, what must he be thinking? Would it be better to think I left him and was alive, or that I was picked up by the SS and enslaved or dead?"

She hardly took a breath. She broke down and stopped talking, though we thought she wanted to say more. There was an emptiness in the pit of my stomach. Separation is terrible, but separation on these terms is worse. I have often contemplated this thought when I was in love with Peter and thought of marriage. In our moments of rapture and in our moments of sparring, the recurring question came to my mind. Which is better – to lose someone you love to death or to lose someone you love because they quit loving you? What a question! If you lose them to death, there is sadness that you may never see them again. The consolation is that they loved you.

If you lose someone you love because they quit loving you, where is the comfort there? I think the hope that they are still alive and may fall back in love with you and return carries you through. But, there is the greater likelihood that they will continue on with someone else. Their life goes on with another love in happiness, while you clutch the air and perfumed scent of their exit. Which is better? I think I would rather lose a loved one to death, knowing they loved me and left me against their will.

If that is the case, how hard for Fredrick? He doesn't have one hope or the other, so he must be struggling with the devastating elements of both options. She left me, doesn't love me, may be dead, and may have died blaming me. Poor Fredrick, indeed. Of course, what are the chances that Fredrick is alive? Surely, he was caught as Hitler's henchmen closed off their ghetto. Then I struggle with how Wilma must cope with this massive mistake. She didn't say it, but if I could finish her mourning; how hard was it for Fredrick to go to the gas chamber feeling no one loved him? How ready he had to be to die, with no reason to live, when the world has turned against him just after his greatest love left him. I don't know how you ever get past that.

I am hurting in here. I am starving in here, as is my sister. The consolation I have that I never realized before is that I am here still loved. My parents didn't leave me. I didn't leave them. I fell more in love with them up to the day we parted. I know they probably loved me so greatly, that they were at love's full capacity of feeling for me and Margot. God has held us together and brought us closer. If we do part, and we are for the moment, at least we have been parted in love.

Yours, Anne M. Frank

Wednesday, November 15, 1944

In all our duties today, I am still thinking of Wilma. I saw her as she headed to her work task and we went to ours after roll call. She seemed more distant, as if she had shared something with us that she should not have shared. She hardly held her head up. I will try to catch her tonight before lights out to encourage her.

As I think of that, I think of Mother. What conversations must she be having in Barrack 29 if she is still there? I pray she knows her daughters love her, and that we realize she did all she could to keep us alive and together. I hope she knows that I, especially I, love her. I want her to know that all my disrespect and outward animosity back in the Annexe was just immature Anne. I pray she knows I grew out of that in time.

Is Mother eating? Is she alive? I hope so. I pray the thought of being reunited will push her ahead. Just to think, she could have been out of Auschwitz early on if only she and Margot would have left me. If she had left, it would be Mother and Margot, and not Margot and me. I know Mother would rather her two daughters be together, supporting each other. This had to have been her goal for us.

"Mother, I hate us being separated. We long to get back to you; to have you here with us. You could make it here, while we seem to be faltering. We do not seem to have the resourcefulness you have. If you were here, I bet we would all be a little more sustained, with a little more bread under our pillows. Please hang on. Wait for us and we will wait for you."

Every transport here, or I should say, every walk-up here, I look for her. I look for her probably as much as the sweet lady looks for Natasha. I will keep looking and hoping. I want our family together. I miss Pim too.

Thursday, November 16, 1944

Dearest Kitty,

I am only fifteen going on forty-five years old. I look back at my life and there have been so many chapters – the Frankfurt years, the Amsterdam years, the Annexe years, the time at Westerbork, the horrific time in Auschwitz, and now the dreadful time here in Bergen-Belsen. How many more chapters in my life will I have? I fear this is the last chapter. My hope is that my life, which began on such a good note, will end on an even better note.

Each morning, we turn the page in this chapter. Each page seems to turn a little slower. Each day there are things to record in this chapter. I pray that I can record all that I have shared with you and one day finish this book. I want to see a compelling historic narrative, and I pray all the players make it through to the end of this project.

Yours, Anne M. Frank

Friday, November 17, 1944

My dearest Kitty,

I had the most frightful dream last night. It makes me afraid to sleep. I can't see her face again. In the dream, Margot and I were picking up trash around the barracks. A piece of paper blew near the outer fence. I was tired and weak, as was Margot. We decided to ignore that we saw it. As we continued moving across the camp, looking down, I bumped into a guard who stepped in front of me out of nowhere. I looked up. He hit me in the face with the cross section of his rifle. I fell back, and he told me, "Turn around, wretch, and get that piece of paper!" I regained my stance. I knew what he was talking about. I had hoped we could let it go.

I turned and walked toward the fence and saw the sweet lady there on the other side of the fence. The paper had been stopped on my side of the fence. As I walked toward her, I dreaded the call, "Natasha, Natasha." There was no way to avoid her. She had the familiar long dress on, but this time, she had some sort of pretty flowered head-cover, like a scarf. She was looking down at the paper that was being restrained by the fence.

As I got nearer, I was haunted by the fact that she stood so lifeless, just staring at the waste, as if expecting it to do something different than just lay vertically, plastered on the wire. I got closer and was about to reach for the trash that I had avoided, when I looked up at her. Her head was still down, and her head-cover was casting a shadow over her face. I could not see her clearly, but there was something about her that was different. Just then, she raised her head. The sunlight cast its revealing beam. It was Mother! With a grief-crackling voice, she cried out, "Anne! Anne! Margot! Margot! Anne! Anne! Margot! Margot!" I swallowed hard and, in the dream, I said, "Mother, it's me. Anne. We're alive. I am right here. Margot is right over there." Again, she cried out, "Anne! Anne! Margot! Margot!" As she took another breath, I said, "Mother, it's me, Anne." She stopped and looked deep into my eyes, at my nose, my mouth, and up and down my body. With a perplexed glance, I knew what the issue was. She did not know me. Mother did not know her own daughter.

It wasn't dementia; she had the look of clarity and comprehension. It wasn't her at all. It was me. I had changed so much in appearance that she could not pick out my identifying characteristics because of the shell of a person I have become. I was horrified. She began to call out, "Anne! Anne! Margot! Margot!" I said, "Mother, it's me! Don't you know me?" And with a guilt-passing plea, she looked me in the face and said, "Will you please help me find my daughters?" She was looking around me, as if I was blocking her view of the other women in camp.

And then I woke up with a cold sweat. I shook Margot in our bunk, trembling. I did not hesitate to wake Margot. We had made an agreement to wake each other up after a nightmare so we could find comfort and a person to hold on to. I wept for an hour or so. Margot just clenched me tight. She kept saying, 'It's alright, Anne. It's alright. I'm here. That wasn't Mother. She knows us both. Hang on, Anne."

Monday, November 20, 1944

My dearest Kitty,

I know you have been worried about me. I have not been able to think or write or speak to you. I am just paralyzed by the dream I had of Mother. And, I am so hungry and so weak.

Margot is not doing well. She had another fainting spell Saturday and seemed to be hallucinating. They put her in the infirmary. Most of the time, if we are sick, we are just left in our barracks because everyone here is sick. Margot's condition got so bad, that they made room for her, and she actually is under a Doctor's care. He has no real medical resources to help, but in a makeshift way, he is treating her.

Someone else has taken her place in our bunk. This new girl is weak too and scared. I don't mind giving her a place as long as she doesn't mind moving over when Margot returns.

Yours, Anne M. Frank

Wednesday, November 22, 1944

Dearest Kitty,

I visit Margot every day. I got so depressed leaving her there today after working with the new girl on our trash detail. Most of us around here still have to work, but we take turns holding each other up. Some are having nervous breakdowns. They can't quit crying. Others can't quit screaming. Worst of all, they leave these hysterical women in our barracks, which only makes the rest of us unsettled.

I have to admit, I want to cry all the time too. I would love, at times, to have one of these guards do me the ultimate favor, but I want to hold out hope for Mother to arrive and for Margot to get well. While I am at it, I would love to see Pim pick us up in the family vehicle and drive us all away. How nice it would be to go out to eat with the Goslars again like when we were young. Hanneli and I could catch up on our gossip. Margot could care for the Goslars' youngest daughter. Perhaps, we would pick up the Van Daans and make an evening of it.

Speaking of Ms. Van Daan. She is here, Kitty. I told her the other day that I would kill for some of her cooking. She said she would kill to have something to cook. I know that's right. We can dream, I told her, as I hunched over from a sharp stomach pain. She said that she understood fully how I feel. I sure wish the Allies would hurry up and break the backs of these oppressors so we can all go home.

Yours, Anne M. Frank

Thursday, November 23, 1944

Dearest Kitty,

Hysteria has hit closer to home. Margot is still in the infirmary. They are getting her what she really needs most, some food. It is very little, as they do not have much for us here. I think even the guards have been reduced from three meals to two. How horrible it must be!

I went for my evening visit. As I got closer, I heard a loud cry from the sick-barrack. I was afraid to go in and wondered who could be making all that racket. It was blood-curdling. I owed it to Margot to go see her, no matter how unnerving it might be. I prepared myself before I entered through the old, beat-up wooden door. I determined that I would not go toward the crying, but would make a left and go straight to Margot's bunk. Surely, this screaming would be upsetting to her as well.

I opened the door. My eyes adjusted. I stepped over a deceased person, and then around another of the dead. The closer I got to Margot's bed, the louder the cry was. "Poor Margot," I thought. "Our barrack is going to look awfully good to her after this." There was a crowd of volunteer nurses around this one bed. I tried to get around them and get to Margot. Then I realized, it was Margot they were holding down. I wanted to vomit. This was not the girl I grew up with. I had never, ever seen anyone this way, and especially not Margot. She was uncontrollable and very strong. It took all of them to hold her down.

Someone said, "It's her sister. Let her through." I got to her, but Margot looked through me, still screaming. I said, "Margot, honey it's me! It's alright Margot. It's alright Margot." I did not know what to do. Finally, I began a familiar prayer that Father would pray with us often in our beds. It was the familiar prayer rhyme that caught her attention. She calmed and began to recite it with me. She released. She lay back and rested, repeating the prayer rhyme over and over, looking up at the ceiling. I sat by her for a long time. The more I looked at my sister, the more depressed and hopeless I felt. She drifted to sleep. The staff didn't say it, but I could tell in their softness that they were grateful.

I walked out into the cool of the evening. I was breaking inside. I walked to the fence where I had once seen that sweet old lady; where I had seen my mother in that nightmare. Neither were there, but what I saw was one of the most startling, beautiful sunsets I had ever seen. I just froze, mystified. "Has it been this long since I have observed God's Creation?" I stood there. A gentle breeze pressed against my skin. It brought with it a sweet cedar or pine aroma, along with the smell of a fresh cut field. A song came to my mind that I had heard years ago. I never remember learning the lyrics, but they came to me so automatically. "This is my Father's world, and to my listening ears; all nature sings, and round me rings, the music of the spheres. This is my Father's world; I rest me in the thought, of rocks and trees, of skies and seas, His Hand the wonders wrought."

Yours, Anne M. Frank

Friday, November 24, 1944

My dearest Kitty,

I had such a good night's sleep. It was almost as if I was back in our home in Amsterdam before the war interrupted our lives. It is so easy to be down and depressed. I know I will be again soon. But, how can anyone blame God for what we are facing. When mankind does what mankind wants with the freedom God has given, against the creeds and laws and statutes He has given, how can the world not end up this way? The commands of God are old, some say outdated, but they are the guide-posts for a peaceful life. If we stay within the guideposts; if we keep on the road that He has laid out for us, there is joy, love, and peace. It's when we think we can violate those sacred laws of what is right and what should be done that all things fall apart. When man trades these in for what is wrong and what should not be done, we experience what we are suffering now. The result of such straying brings countless numbers of victims and inconceivable collateral damage.

It reassures me to know that as we are suffering and weeping, Pim would be weeping too if he saw this. Pim would do all he could to make things right and protect us. If Pim, our earthly father, would grieve over this, how much more our Heavenly Father? How many times is He cry-ing out for this to stop? How often is He crying out to the Allies to stop the Nazi killing machine and working to make it stop? It is amazing to think that as pieces on a chess board, God is working through the players, who belong to the light, to offset, obstruct, and remove the powers of darkness.

I am thinking of what I just shared with you, Kitty. I have got to remember to tell this to Margot. She is going to flip to see I can think theologically just like her at times!

Yours, Anne M. Frank

Saturday, November 25, 1944

Dearest Kitty,

I woke up this morning using the end of my blanket as an elevation for my head. It's not necessarily a pillow, but you take what you have. Anyway, when I woke up, I had my blanket covering me and the end folded for my head. I laid my hands, clasped as in prayer under my head, on top of the blanket roll. As I got up, I saw a few crumbs fall out from under that corner of the blanket. Normally, one would not notice that, but here in the starvation camp, every crumb counts. I wondered if some crumbs had fallen off the side of my mouth from some bread I had eaten. How could that be? I have not eaten in a few days. I felt under the knotted corner of my blanket. There was a piece of bread – about the size of my two fingers! This was so odd. I looked around. I wondered if this was from my bunkmate, but I dared not to ask in case it was hers.

The more I wondered what to do with it, the more guilty I felt. Here I was thinking of man doing what man wants to do and seeing awful results, and I want to keep what belongs to someone else because I am in need. I knew if I asked her, she would say it was hers, whether it was or not. Who wouldn't in our present state? Idiot Anne asked anyway. I prayed first, and then I asked. You'll never guess what she said. By the way, her name is Lydia. I generally never get their names anymore because people are in and out of here so quickly. They come in barely walking and leave feet first. It's better if you don't know anyone's name, but we never ever want to know their number. I asked her, "Lydia, I found this. Is it yours?" She licked her lips, and her eyes looked as if she had seen a Christmas turkey. She answered honestly, "Anne, it's not, but I wish it was." I asked her, "It's new found bread, so would you like to share it with me?" She was glad to do so.

It wasn't much, but what a surprise. Who would leave bread under my created-pillow? I must have been sound asleep. I looked around. No one gave me a smile, or a nod or an acknowledgement of a kind deed. I guess it's a mystery. I pray we have more of them.

Yours, Anne M. Frank

Monday, November 27, 1944

Dearest Kitty,

Margot and I are back together again. It's not what you think. We are back together in the infirmary. I passed out in the yard Sunday. I was feeling dizzy, kind of like when you jump up too fast from lying down. I thought it would pass, but then I felt the ground pulling me to itself. I was powerless. I woke up on the cold, hard ground and saw a guard, as well as some ladies, standing over me. By the way, the guard's name is Izzo. That is appropriate because he "is so" mean. He swore at me a few times, and then ordered me up. I tried to, at his command. I was just too weak. Izzo then told the other ladies to carry me to the infirmary or to the pit, whichever they chose. Thankfully, they didn't take me to the pit where the bodies are thrown. I landed in bed near Margot. They got me some water and bread, and I just laid there in and out of sleep all day.

I felt better today. Margot has been doing so much better since her emotional breakdown. We lay there and talked about how life has changed. She knew my ambitions and that this was nowhere in the realm of where either of us thought our lives would be. Margot then commented that it is odd. She said, "We lay here in bed, Jewish girls." Having studied religion, our heritage, and our faith, Margot drew a very interesting analogy. She reminded me of the ten plagues in Egypt. She said of the ten plagues, we had experienced all ten in one way or another:

In the first plague, the water turned to blood and the Egyptians could not drink the water. Here, we have little water to drink, and what we have is not fit to drink.

The second plague: frogs covered the land. We have rats covering ours.

The third plague was lice. We have experienced this literally.

The fourth plague: swarms of flies. We have flies all over our dead and diseased.

The fifth plague: there was a pestilence of their livestock and their cows were dying left and right from disease. I would not doubt the bombs have taken care of most of our livestock. The Germans saved the rest for their officers to eat.

The sixth plague was the plague of boils on the skin. We have struggled constantly with scabies.

The seventh plague was thunder, lightning, and hail which fell on the earth killing livestock and people, plants and trees. We have seen this plague. The thunder and lightning of war has dominated the horizon. The bombs have fallen on our cities and countryside, demolishing structures and land.

The eighth plague was locusts devouring the land. We have seen this in two ways. The fleas eat us up in our barracks. Beyond that, the Nazis have devoured everything we value, taking it for themselves.

The ninth plague was darkness over all the land. We have seen the darkness of humanity. We have been forced to work under the dark cloud, go to barracks where each morning we are faced with darkness of another day.

The tenth plague that set the Israelites free was when the firstborn children of the Egyptians were killed. We have seen our firstborn killed, our second-born, our third-born, and our next-born.

What is so dramatic about what Margot was sharing with me was that God was doing this to the Egyptians because of the way they were treating our people. When these events occurred, the Israelites were in the land of Goshen, spared from every one of these plagues. We had to discuss this at length. We are the Israelites. We have been sold into slavery again. We have been abused again. We have been devalued as humans again. We have been made to be working livestock and nothing better. We have had our children killed because they believe we are too many. How many babies were killed at Auschwitz? How many mothers, who were able to pass by the first selection pregnant, carried to term and delivered, just to have their babies drown before their eyes in a bucket of water? How many other pregnant women were kicked and beaten until they miscarried? And the most horrible of notions; how many did Mengele experiment on? We had heard he was doing some heinous things those last days.

Here was our debate. We were the offended. We are the Israelites who are being abused and yet the Germans are not receiving the plagues of Egypt. We are! Where is our land of Goshen? Where is our exemption from these plagues? We both just laid back after an exhausting time of trying to understand. We don't understand. We do believe Germany is losing the war, along with their Axis co-conspirators. The two of us in this sick bed also feel we are losing too.

After a long time of silence, Margot had one last thing to say before we went to sleep. She said that God said to Moses somewhere in the Book of Exodus, "I have heard the groaning of the children of Israel, and I will bring you out with My outstretched arm." I told her, "I sure wish God would hurry. What are we to do until then?" Margot had an answer for this; she said that God spoke through the Prophet Isaiah to say, "Fear thou not; for I am with thee: be not dismayed; for I am thy God: I will strengthen thee; yea, I will help thee; yea, I will uphold thee with the right hand of my righteousness."

I wondered where this confidence was the other day when Margot was beside herself screaming, uncontrollably? She was soothed when we quoted a prayer rhyme from Pim. I wonder? Did she turn to God and to all her studies about Him to bring her such insights and relative peace? I don't know, Kitty, but I sure am finding comfort in this Margot.

Yours, Anne M. Frank

Tuesday, November 28, 1944

Well Kitty,

Margot and I got evicted! They threw us out of the infirmary. They said that there were people much sicker than us who needed this extra attention. Of course, my question was, "What extra attention? We get fed every other day as opposed to every third day? Oh, they spoil us! It would be comical if it weren't so serious." Besides all that, can one person be deader than another? Dead is dead. In here, sick is sick. We all are on the cusp of death. It hardly seems possible to differentiate one being sicker than another, especially when there are no exams. I guess they just eyeball us and say, "These two people look closer to death than you two, so move out!"

We are back in our old barrack. Some new women took our bunk, so now we are at the very front of our barrack, right in front of the door. That is the bunk no one wants because the cold wind blows in. With so many women in here, and so many in and out to go to the restroom, or to drag their dead mate out of the building, the cold air just blows right in on us. We aren't well, but most of that is from lack of food. When it gets really cold, we will have a time of it in this spot. We don't pray for anyone to die in a more favorable part of the building. It would be nice though, if some moved out and let us move back.

We were given light duty today. They gave us a rusted needle and some tangled thread and ordered us to sew up holes in the clothes of the late-residents. When someone dies, they strip them naked, and throw them outside. It is cold enough that they last for a few days. Once the decay gets too bad, some of our other mates are ordered to load the diseased cadavers, we call people, and take them to the pit. If they are wrapped in a blanket, they are rolled out of that blanket so others can enjoy its warmth. This is so nasty because of the smell, but if we have to choose between cold and smell, we choose smell. This is how sub-human, base animals we have become. I do not like what I am becoming. Survival is all that seems to matter. We push and fight, elbow and punch to get an extra bite of bread.

What is even worse, it seems Margot and I have only each other in this whole place. We are the youngest in our barrack, and perhaps the youngest in our whole wing of this camp. I don't know if that plays a part. It seems that all the other ladies avoid us. I know they are older, and I am sure their life experiences are different. There is more water under the bridge for them, I suppose. I asked one why they always got quiet when we were around. The lady said, "Pay no attention to that. It's not you. We just don't relate to girls your age." That is an answer, I guess. I wonder if they get irritated that we fight for our food, that we refuse to just let them take and take. It is nice to let the elders eat first, but in this setting, if you don't grab first, you get nothing. It is best to fight for our share of the meager offerings, so that all can have some. The alternative is they get a little more and we die. This makes no sense when the extra they get is so little that it does them no good. We get our share, which is so little. Our needs are not met, but we gain an extra hour or day of life.

Wednesday, November 29, 1944

Dearest Kitty,

In one of my favorite pastimes of reading about celebrities, I was able to learn about American actors and actresses. They live really lavish lives. They live in standards that rival our monarchs. I love to read about how they celebrate Thanksgiving. The who's who of fame come to their homes with their families. They have a huge turkey that they carve up and eat along with all the side dishes. They eat all they can and there is still plenty left. They go and sit on the divan, smoke a cigar, play some board game, and talk about how they will never eat again.

I am not sure if today is Thanksgiving back in the United States, but I am sure their holiday is not far away. They are eating scrumptious meals, while we would beg for crumbs from our oppressors' tables. I get angry at myself for following the stars. I have followed them. They could follow me and people like me who are suffering. They know what is going on over here, yet no one seems to lift a finger. They eat knowing, most likely, that we can't. Why won't they do without all that, pray, and take on the honorable mission to liberate us?

I walked out of the barrack after a drink of unclean water, filled with the backwash of my peers. I went to the fence and gazed at the wintering grass rising up on the hill behind us. I imagined that was all spinach. I thought of how I could graze that wonderful field, and grow strong as Popeye (the fictitious character created the same year I was born). With that strength, I would overpower the guards, lift the fence, and me and Margot and about ten thousand more of us would leave, never to return.

I can also see that field covered in lettuce. We used to eat boiled lettuce all the time in the Annexe. I complained the whole time. Little did I know how valuable our food cycles were. What I wouldn't give to eat the same things, over and over again. I thought going hungry would be better. Now, I know hunger. It is not better.

Yours, Anne M. Frank

Thursday, November 30, 1944

My dearest Kitty,

I caught Margot doing an odd thing today. Of course, as time passes, we are all going odd. She was laying on the ground, on her back, around midday. I thought she had passed out again and I dropped my bag (we are back on the trash crew). "Margot, are you alright?" I asked. She said, "Yes Anne. Lay down beside me." The ground was dry for once, and so I laid down just a moment beside her. In our condition, we don't want to lie still long. They will see our emaciated bodies and cart us to the pit.

There was a beautiful blue sky with the whitest of clouds just in clusters all over the blue canvas. The clouds took up half the sky and were so billowy, like huge, fluffy cotton balls or white, happy, fat lambs. She asked me, "Do you see that?" I asked her, "Do you mean the clouds and the beautiful display?" She said, "Yes. There are so many clustered together. Please stay with me in what I am about to say. Those clouds in that sky remind me of a day when I saw the smoke rising from the crematorium in Auschwitz. I looked at the smoke covering the sky, and for a minute, I thought the smoke was almost as beautiful as the clouds on a sunny day. I have noticed that artists always paint skies with clouds. For some reason, clouds add extra beauty and character. Before I could catch myself, I began to admire the majestic feel of those clouds of smoke blowing over the camp. Then I shuddered at what I was doing. That smoke was not beautiful bodies of moisture trapped, but robbed bodies of people being destroyed."

I said, "Margot, you are not lifting my spirits with this talk." She continued to explain, "Here it is different. We can admire the blue sky with its billowing clouds traveling with a fresh breeze. No one is being gassed or burned here. That's something to be thankful for."

What a weird observation. She was right though. We could admire the clouds, the billows of the heaven above rather than the terrors of earth below. Both filled the sky. One was from above and one was from below. It was God's creation and man's destruction. Here they don't kill us, they just let us die. I don't think it is much more humane this way, but at least the sky is untarnished.

Yours, Anne M. Frank

Saturday, December 2, 1944

Dearest Kitty,

Margot and I are saying our prayers together each night. She really has changed since her event in the infirmary. She is becoming more outspoken and thoughtful. She is also showing more initiative. We prayed for Mother and Father, not knowing if it will do them any good or not. We pray nonetheless. We prayed for the end of the war. We prayed for liberation. We prayed for health. We prayed for food. We prayed for our camp to be more kind to us and to each other. We prayed last night especially for food.

This morning, I woke up to the harsh orders of a new Kapo. I pushed myself up on my Anne-made pillow. I felt something crunch. I got goosebumps all over. Don't let it be a rat or a roach! I was afraid to look. I elbowed Margot and whispered, "There's something under my pillow." She said, "See what it is." I said, "You see. I found it. The least you can do is look." She has changed, but not that much. She refused. I stood far away, with Margot even farther behind me. I reached forward. With one quick flick, I tossed the blanket corner.

Do you know what it was? A piece of bread! It was about the size of three fingers. Margot looked at me. I looked at her. We looked around. No one looking at us. No one glancing around a corner to watch our reactions to this surprise. To be honest, I don't think anyone here likes us enough to leave us bread. Only Mother would do that for us, and she's not here.

I told Margot that this happened once before. She asked, "What did you do? I told her, "I ate it! And, I shared a piece with the girl who replaced you." "Was it any good", she asked. I said, "It was stale, but it was edible. Do you want to share this with me?" Margot said, "Yes, but you first." She is such a coward. I ate it. She ate her part. It was bread. That's all I can say. It met a need. Question; who left it? I still wonder who turned us in at the Annexe. That was bad. Now I wonder who is leaving us bread. This is good.

Yours, Anne M. Frank

Sunday, December 3, 1944

Dearest Kitty,

Margot woke me up in the middle of the night. She had a dream. Per our agreement, she nudged me to share her nightmare. She said we were picking up trash on the compound near the gate. The guard motioned, and the gate was opened. In came a big army truck. Margot said she did not recognize the insignia of the truck at first, but could tell it was not German. When the truck pulled closer, she thought it was a Russian troop-transport truck. When the driver door opened, out stepped a woman in military fatigues. It was Mother!

Margot said Mother called out to both of us, "Margot, Anne, get in the truck. I am taking you out of here! She said that in the dream, we kept asking questions, "How did you get here? How did you get out? How did you get a Russian truck?" Mother said she would answer all those questions later, but for now, get in the truck. We kept asking her about Father, but she said, "Father will meet us where we are going." We climbed in. Margot said though in the dream she was in the truck; she was able to also see the truck from a third-party perspective drive out of the gate. She said that just as it passed out of the gate, it disappeared. The guards looked aghast, and the prisoners in our camp began to cry. Margot wept slightly too as she was telling me, "What can it mean Anne?"

I was taken aback at her grief. I told her that I didn't see this as a nightmare but an answer to our prayers. We were rescued. We were able to leave this place and were rejoined with Mother, and Father was soon to meet us. How can that be sad? It also gave me hope that there is life after this torment and that we will be together as a family again. Margot was just upset that we disappeared. I have to admit, I don't know what this would mean. I hope it means we disappear out of the enemy's clutches, and that the other prisoners cried because they wanted to go with us too.

We decided to hold on to our dreams and remember them. Who knows? Maybe the good dreams will come true for all of us. It is the only thing that sustains us here. There are times that I wish I could stay asleep and dream. This would pass the time. Besides, the more I am in the dream-state, the less I am here in this misery-state.

Yours, Anne M. Frank

Monday, December 4, 1944

Dearest Kitty,

There just can't be that much trash in a place where there is no food, no parcels, and no Red Cross packages. I don't believe I have ever seen a Red Cross package, but I hear the prisoners on the other side of the Star Camp (where the Jews with stars on their clothes are) get Red Cross packages weekly. They are better fed over there, but even the SS troops sift through their packages, taking out choice food, and then passing the rest on to the people.

With that said, we scour this place for trash. The guards throw some of their trash on the ground to give us something to do. They are also bad about hiding trash. When we say we are finished, they will ask us, "Are you sure, wretches? Look again. Don't come back until you have had a good long look." We go and sometimes we find a piece of trash placed between two rocks. Other times we miss the well-hidden trash. They then call us names, curse us, grab us by the skin and bone arms, and drag us to some trash they had hidden. They then make us pick it up. When we bend down, they kick us the rest of the way down. When one of us objects, the guard knocks the other of us down. I think this is why we have become programmed to just stand by when a loved one is mistreated. What good does it do either of us if we are both decommissioned. Then who will take care of us?

When we had been cleared of our duties today, we went back to the barrack, which is as cold inside as it is outside. The only benefit of going to our barrack is that at least it blocks the wind. The more of us that are in there, the less cold it becomes. My teeth were chattering today. Margot was shivering. We sat on our bunk with the two others that have joined us there and spoke of our hunger, our cold, and our worries. It is the same conversation every day. I told them that I am tired of this talk. It makes things no better. We are all in agreement that we are hungry and cold, so the discussion isn't a debate to persuade one over to another opinion. I told them about Peter and me in the Annexe. I even shared some things with the ladies that Margot didn't even know. I wanted to get them tickled, so I told them about how Peter described the male genitalia, and how I told him, in depth, about the female genitalia. They were rolling in laughter. Of course, these two in our bunks were familiar first hand with all these things, but not me and Margot. Our knowledge was just about our own and from the books we had read about such matters. One of our bunkmates chuckled and asked, "There was no show and tell

involved, was there?" I blushed, "Certainly not!." Margot looked relieved, as we all giggled like school girls. Finally, some humor from four
corpse-frail women. I pictured four skeletons all rattling their bones in
delight about something the other said.

I then told them that we believe that sex is for marriage only. That
led me to the discussion of my wedding. Margot and I had not spoken
much about our dream weddings in a long time. Margot wants a private,
family affair. Of course, she does. That's Margot. I want a big wing-ding.
I want friends from school, people from the neighborhood, Father and
Mother's friends and neighbors. I want Miep, Bep, Jan, Mr. Kugler, Mr.
Kleinman, and Mr. Voskuijl there. I would welcome the Van Daans and
even Dussel, provided he stay out of the toilet and not irritate me with
his selfish behavior or with his rocking back and forth during our prayer.
I want Father to give me away. I can see his sweet arm around mine. We
walk down the aisle together. I see all these heads turned to look at me.
I notice they glance at me and then they look at Pim. Women begin to
cry. We get near the front of the wedding chapel and I look at Pim just in
time to see him wipe away the tears from his eyes with his free hand. He
raises my veil to kiss me on the cheek, and then lowers the veil back to
its place. He takes my hand and transfers my care from him to my groom.
Tears began to roll down my eyes just telling this, and again as I recount
this to you, Kitty.

Then the question, of course, came, "Who will be your groom?" I
told them it could be a Peter, but my preference is Peter Schiff. I did
acknowledge that I most likely have never met the man that I will marry.
I do know he is going to be wonderful. He will stand on his own two feet.
He will love Father and Mother. He will want children, lots of children.
He will have a good job and be strong, not needing to lean on me. He will
have Father's personality and business acumen. He will provide fine
clothing for me and give me his full attention. He will also notice how

many men look at me, and he will get jealous about it. I will like that. He cannot take me for granted.

Now, please know, he will want to support me, but he will not have to. I am going to be a writer and make lots of money on my own. He will run his business, but he will seek my input. He will be chairman of the board, but I will always be on the board of his business, as will other women. Business needs the female touch. God has given us male and female. The man needs a helpmate.

I was thinking of how opposite Father and Mother are. I was also thinking back at Mother's resourcefulness in camp and how much Father would have benefitted from having Mother involved in his business. Then I came back to the thought of how opposite they are. I told this to the group. I had their full attention! Now, don't get me wrong, Kitty, I did let them talk too, but this is my diary.

A thought came to me, so I pressed my skinny elbows against my side, just below my ribs, which are easily discernable. I extended my fore-arms straight out, with my hands pointing straight forward, left palm facing right palm, right palm facing left palm. I told them that I see marriage like my hands. They face in opposite directions. My left hand faces right. My right-hand faces left. I told them that they are total opposites. I then brought my hands together in a prayer grasp, alternating fingers. I said, "Look how good two opposites come together. If the left hand and right hand faced the same direction, they could not come together very easily. Because they are opposites, they function so much better together. I think that's what marriage is. Two opposites coming together. Where one is weak, the other is strong. Where one sees things from one view-point, the other sees things from the other viewpoint. Together they are complete." One of the other ladies wrapped around me and said, "I love you, Anne! That is such a great analogy. You bring light to this dark place." That was sweet to hear! I hope that is what my life will be.

Yours, Anne M. Frank

Tuesday, December 5, 1944

Yesterday ended on such a good note. Today began on a bad note. Such opposites I cannot stand. One of the two ladies visiting with us yesterday after work did not wake up this morning. The Kapos called us out of bed. On the bed, there lies Margot, then me, then Beatrice, and then Elizabeth. Margot rose. I rose. Elizabeth rose. But between me and Elizabeth, Beatrice lay still. I nudged her but felt the cold, stiff body. Chill bumps covered me. So, this is how this goes. When will I not wake up? It is hard to get up already. Each of us is just a hair short of where Beatrice is now.

They ordered us out. Then the death crew of prisoners went through each barrack hauling out the dead. I fear there will be more of this to come if our liberation is delayed. They throw them out in stacks in front of the barrack. A light snow is falling. How tragic. Beatrice and others were still in front of our barracks when we returned. It's as if they want to get a certain number in front before they haul them to the pit. I guess they figure it is better to hit a certain quota for the dead to make it worth their while to carry the load to the pit. If they take each dead person, they will make lots of trips. If they get enough at a time, they can stack them in the wheelbarrow and reduce their number of trips. This is unfeeling to say, but I think the death crew, which is made up of prisoners like us, are wise to conserve their energy. I wonder how many want to wheel the dead to the pit, dump the wheelbarrow, and then climb in with the bodies down below, hoping to pull the dirt over on top of them?

Needless to say, we had a lot of people cursing God today. The guards do it as a sport. The majority of prisoners do it with contempt. God is still being blamed. As long as I live, I will never curse God. How can I? He is my only refuge. He is our only hope. If we can't pray to Him, then who can help us. Who do we pray to? We are powerless on our own. No positive thinking is going to help us here. Positive thinking is just an internal lie.

We are Jewish, and yet I feel we are different from all other Jews in history. The Jews before us were brutalized, beaten, enslaved, and killed. From what I can tell and remember from my reading, they never blamed God for Pharaoh. They never blamed God for Haman. They never blamed God for Antiochus Epiphanes. They cried out to God to change the circumstance, and to remove these murderers. Jews were killed then too, but God came through. I still believe He will do the same now. He is my hope, not the British, not the Americans, not the Dutch, and certainly not the Russians. So, we wait.

PS. Today, if we were back in Holland, we would be celebrating Sinterklaas. We would lay a shoe out by the window and hope that Sinterklaas or his Zwarte Pieten (his helpers, the Black Peters) would leave us some gifts. We were told that the Zwarte Pieten keep records of our good and bad deeds in a big book. They then reward us accordingly. If we have been good, they leave us wonderful gifts. If we have been bad, the legend is, they would take us to Spain for a year to teach us how to be good. At this point, either would be acceptable. I believe that I have been good. How else could I be any different? We have no control and very little opportunity to do bad. I would gladly wake up in the morning and find bread in my shoe. But if I have been bad (I have had some bad thoughts for sure), I would gladly go to Spain to learn some lessons. Anything is better than this. I miss Father and Mother. I miss being a child again with Margot. We were so safe, so protected, and so cared for. We can't go back, but in my mind, I frequent those times again and again. It is a respite to this living nightmare. I have found reminiscing to be a glorious escape.

Wednesday, December 6, 1944

My dearest Kitty,

I wish we could forage for food. I imagine being out in a forest, perhaps lost, or have a camping trip go bad. I could also imagine myself in the army (fighting for the Allies, of course). In the woods, food would grow short. What would we do? We would forage. We would make do with what we could get. We would hunt for edible berries, for naturally growing greens, or for edible fruit from some tree. We would fish for our meal or hunt for our dinner. We would trap animals too. Whatever it took, we would do it. The beauty of a forest is you can forage for food. But, we are stuck here in a camp, surrounded by barbed wire, guard towers, machine guns, and electric fences. The only foraging we have is to forage in here. We have nothing to forage for. If it was here, it is not now. If it were edible, we have eaten it already. What do we do? Why are the Nazis holding us here? We are not helping the war effort for them because we do not produce anything. We are not helping them with some prisoner exchange because no one wants us. All these prison camps are doing is taking up rations from their war effort, withholding men from their front lines. Why keep us here? Why not let us go?

We can't join the war effort. We might not live even if freed, as sick as we are. It makes absolutely no sense. If we are here so Hitler can kill us, then why doesn't he kill us. Again, we are caught in a purgatory. I guess the only benefit of having us here is to torture us with a slow death. If you hate someone so badly, this would be the way you would exact the utmost, vengeful satisfaction.

I could easily see paying these back for what they are doing to us. What would I do to get back at them? I would put them through the same torment. I would have a gas chamber at the end of the prison and randomly order people to their deaths, leaving their family members barely alive to grieve. I would have a crematorium to burn their bodies at the end of the camp, so their families and my captured guests could experience the fear, the separation, the death, and the burning of the bodies. If I were exacting my revenge, I would starve them, have them do pointless work, shave their heads, dehumanize them, snatch their babies from their arms, and make them watch as I led them off to their death, smiling as I walked. I would live my life in luxury and go back daily to their cage to inflict some more punishment. I would let their cage be just in view of life going on all around them so they could know what they are missing, and that nobody outside cared for them on the inside. I would do this if I were of that sort. I can't even think this way because it is so evil. This is what only the devil would do and those who gleefully call upon his name. This is not what God would do. Thus, we can know that there is a God and there is a devil. There is good. There is evil. Good is fighting evil. God is engaging the devil. We hear the warplanes, the bombs, and the gunfire. God is engaging the devil. He is moving among men to rid mankind of such poison.

How glorious is this confirmation that the evil we see is not of God? I know He is with us here. Because He is here, we can face the lions like Daniel. Because He is here, we can face the fiery furnace like Shadrach, Meshach, and Abed-nego. Because He is here, we can face the giant, Goliath, with a tiny slingshot. Because He is here, we can face our blindness and the sapping of our strength, like Samson. I pray God will rise up against these, so we can rise up and live.

Yours, Anne M. Frank

Saturday, December 9, 1944

Dearest Kitty,

Margot and I decided to forage at a different place today. On the opposite side of our barracks, there was a barbed wire fence with straw and wood tied between to prevent one side from seeing the other. This was the area where we were told Red Cross packages with food were being delivered. I am not sure why they get special treatment. We were forbidden to go to that fence or visit with those on the other side. I suppose it is because they don't want one side to know what the other side is or isn't getting. During the day, the guards walk among us, but at night, they go to their own living spaces. Only the guards in the towers watch over us. It is at night that we can go to that fence and try to make contacts. The barracks hide the view of all guard towers but one, and he is far enough away that the shadow covers our foray.

I remember saying in the Annexe that when you are hungry, anything will do. I will go one step farther, and say when you are hungry, you will do anything. We could not see the lady prisoners on the other side. However, through the cracks, their outlines, illuminated by the exterior fence lights, broadcast shadows on our side of the ground. I am sure our shadows from the fence lights behind us cascade across their ground too. This lets us know when someone is on the other side of the fence near us. In a hushed whisper, we ask them if they have any food. They ask who we are, where we are from, and what our conditions are. We tell them how hungry we are. Now, we could be lying to get their food for our own surplus, but they have heard clearly that we are being neglected like the worst of animals. They, at times, toss some food over. If any of the prisoners on our side see food coming over, they rally to that place and all of us fight for whatever comes over.

When Pim would take us to the park, we would throw some bread on the ground. The ducks would all scurry to get their piece of the bread. One day, I had an ice cream cone. I had finished the ice cream and didn't want the pointy end of the cone. I asked Father if the ducks would eat an ice cream cone. He told me to give it a try. I threw it down. Just like that, fifty ducks fell on it in our midst. They tried to each get a part, but then one duck flew in and grabbed the whole cone. He got it on his beak and it looked like the cone had become an extra-large beak on his tiny head. He was going to keep the cone for himself. He tried to get away and the birds fell into a scrum upon him. We were shocked, but that duck was able to keep his wits and my cone. With extra effort, he lifted off the ground with that cone and flew over the other side of the creek that fed the pond. The rest of the ducks looked at us as if to ask, "Are you going to let him get away with that? That was mean of him to take the ice cream cone you gave to all of us." They looked so hurt. We just laughed and watched that one strong, selfish duck have a feast day on that ice cream cone.

This is exactly what we are doing in our starvation side of camp. Life is imitating nature. Women are copying ducks. Food comes over, and we all huddle around it. No one really cares to share unless there are sisters or mothers and daughters in the mix. Every night, we do the same thing. It is work. It is hard. It isn't fair. It is every woman for herself. But, it is all we can do, so we do what we have to. Finally, we have found another source of food, as scant as it may be. Each night, if we have strength, we make it to the fence. There are days nothing is thrown over to us. When the Red Cross trucks arrive, the news comes to us fast, and we all meet at the fence for the next few nights.

On days when there is no food, we get bored and go and sit near the fence, where we see a shadow. There, in the midnight hours, we visit with the unseen person on the other side. It is strange, but it is easier to talk to the people we cannot see than the people we can see. I suppose we are able to be more honest. Seldom are names exchanged there. We talk of our families, of our arrests, or of our journey to get to this place in our lives. We confess some sins we have committed and mistakes we wish we could undo. Then, one of us gets tired, gets up, and returns to our barracks. Sometimes, the lady you are talking to has left long before you realize it. I will be talking and talking (as is my custom), and after a while of silence on the other side, I will ask, "Are you awake?" Nothing. "Are you there?" I ask. Nothing. They just get up for whatever reason and leave. No offense taken. We are all struggling outside and inside.

Yours, Anne M. Frank

Sunday, December 10, 1944

Dearest Kitty,

A massive march of people was heard this morning, moving to the orders of some loud-mouthed commanding officer. Some were walking. Others were being carried. They came in by the thousands. Bodies were stacked by the gate to be carried by our local grave crew when the number reached their required minimum. That occurred sooner than they expected and by many more than they had been accustomed to. Wheelbarrows from all over camp gathered at the gate. Prisoners in stripes loaded them and off to the pit they went. Every barrack on our side was pushed together for more to be allowed in. The SS troops pulled bodies out of our barracks of those who had not been accounted for at roll call. Yes, we still have roll call. More bodies are thrown at the doors of the barracks. Then a camp guard will call out, "We have room here for forty more." Another would answer, "I can top that, I have room for forty-seven here." They were commended for their resourcefulness and hard work.

Sadly, some they threw out were not dead yet. They were just slow-moving because of ill-health. Others would not wake, but they were still breathing. One officiant caught that. He said, "Wait a minute, this one is still alive!." His counterpart recoiled, "Come on man, she won't be that way long." He's right. Keep water from these for a while, and no one can last.

More and more they came in. I wondered, "Where are all these people coming from?" Margot didn't know, nor did Elizabeth. That night at the fence, we heard from the Red Cross part of camp, versus the Red Star side, that the war was going poorly for the Nazis. They were being pushed back on every side. We have heard they have almost been pushed back to Germany proper and are viciously fighting to retain their own country. Serves them right! They came and took over European countries, planting their men in every province, much like the Romans of old. They deserve to have to fight for their homes like we have had to fight and lose ours. As the Germans are losing ground, they are requiring death marches for the prisoners they still hold, abandoning front-line concentration camps. Some new residents in our barrack stated as much.

How terrible are their stories? They are forced to march in step with the well-fed Germans. If one of the starving camp members falls behind, he is beaten. If he doesn't then keep up, he is shot. If one falls to the ground, she is shot. If anyone looks like they can't go any farther, they are shot. When the march slows, they force the healthier prisoners to dig trenches and bury the dead and the near dead.

Every once in a while, we hear the battle near us here. Will they march us too? Margot and I are not strong enough to endure such; nor are most of the women here. How I pray we don't have to flee here. I just want a British tank to pull up at our gate, fire one warning shot, ram the gates, and set us free. They can imprison the Nazis, kill them, or let them run. I just want us out of here. I am still looking for Mother to pull up in that truck that Margot dreamt about.

Yours, Anne M. Frank

Monday, December 11, 1944

Dearest Kitty,

I once complained about how crowded the Annexe was and how little space we had. I was mad because I had to share a room with one other person. I wasn't sharing my bed with Dussel, just my room. I hated sharing that table with him. I hated sharing two and a half floors with eight people. Now, I share a bed with six or eight, sometimes ten. I share a small living quarter with hundreds. I hated our little toilet that the eight of us once shared, and now I have to share a pot or a wheelbarrow with hundreds more, and that is just in my barrack. In the Annexe, we had to share our food and Dussel would always keep some back. The Van Daans ate the best that we had, and kept the best that they had for their three family members (though Peter would sneak me some). Now we share our bread with twenty and thirty. When I say bread, I mean one or two slices of bread. We are living on crumbs and sometimes without crumbs. We fight the rat who grabs a piece of bread, capture him with our blanket, steal back our bread crumb, and then others fight over the rat. What have we become?

We are all striving to be "survivors." Whoever lives through this, wins. Whoever dies in this, loses. That would make sense, but we are battling another mindset. Are we really winners if we live through this? It is a rational question. If I live through this, will I ever regain my health? If I live through this, who will there be to share my life with? Where will we live? Are we to assume our home in Amsterdam will be waiting for us? Is there even a chance our home, or even Father's warehouse that he rented will still be standing after the bombardment?

If we live through this, how will we get back to our home towns? Do we really have a home town? I wanted Holland to be my home, but after the betrayals, can I trust those people again ? Even if I can trust them, will I be able to forgive them for causing the loss of my wonderful father? I don't have a complete education. I have never been able to graduate. I have no job skills other than writing, but who wants a sickly Jewish girl scarred from her bondage to write for them? Our family assets have been taken. Our valuables were picked up by the Gestapo at the Annexe. Two years before, when we had fled to the Annexe, I am sure the Dutch police absconded our furniture and appliances. Could we go live with relatives? Who knows if Grandma is still alive ? Can we hope that Father's brothers or sister has survived; much less, Mother's family? There are so many questions left to answer. I hope that when this is over, there will be a hand leant to help us who have been victimized by the Nazi atrocities. Surely, they will. If God has taken care of us thus far, will He not care for us when this is all over?

Margot and I talked about this before bedtime yesterday evening. We are both longing to be rescued from this. In Jewish culture and religion, there is this longing and hope for God to send His Messiah as He has promised; to regather the Jews and to re-establish the nation of Israel in her homeland. To us, it is a future hope that is reassured because God has promised. There is no idea of when this will occur. I guess this is where so many Jewish people get so disheartened and discouraged. We have heard and recited the Promise for so many generations, for thousands of years, and we are still looking. I think this is why most have turned to self-improvement and self-reliance because this hope has faded to a "legend" or a "mythology." I know about mythologies. I loved to read about them, but I always could tell the difference between these created gods and the Creator God.

Margot remembered a verse from Isaiah that has become one we have decided to hold to. Again, she doesn't remember where it is found, somewhere in the Isaiah 60s she thinks; it says something like, "The Spirit of the Lord God is upon me; because the Lord hath anointed me to preach good tidings to the meek; to bind up the brokenhearted, to declare liberty to the captives, and to open the prisons of the ones imprisoned. And that God will bring vengeance on those who afflict us." That verse or verses really brought an amazing hope to us both. I was getting goosebumps hearing this. I wanted to learn that for my own sake. We spent the next hour or so with her reciting it part by part and me repeating it bit by bit. The bad thing was, Margot said it differently each time, so it was hard to memorize a verse that kept changing. Regardless, I got the gist of it. I am ready to hear the good news. I am ready to have my heart bound up and my imprisoned body to be set free. I am ready to hear liberty declared for me and Margot.

"Oh Lord, please come soon. If You don't, or if it is not time, please send someone to do Your bidding in answer to our prayers. The Israelites cried out to You in Egypt. God, You heard their prayers. Please hear mine tonight."

Yours, Anne M. Frank

Wednesday, December 13, 1944

Dearest Kitty,

I have to tell you about a funny transaction I saw tonight at the fence. One of the new ladies transported in was starving. It didn't take her long to hear of the food at the wire. She went with the rest of us. In her clothes, she had some currency from Hungary. She was walking up and down the fence trying to find someone who could understand one of the broken languages she spoke. I understood some of her words, but not all the time. The Red Cross had not come in a few weeks, so clearly the people on the other side were out of food or had shared all they could spare.

Finally, she found someone. She was trying to offer her money for bread. While the rest of us try to get food through goodwill, she felt she had an advantage. She had cash money. Their conversation went like this:

The lady she engaged said, "I have no food to spare. I am sorry."

The Hungarian woman: "But I have money for you. These others don't. I can give you money that will benefit you for a long time to come. I have enough to give you for several weeks. The SS didn't search me. I hid it in various places under my clothes and in my shoes."

After much pleading, the woman on the other side of the fence had a piece of bread and said, "I will give it to you for three bills of your currency."

The Hungarian woman asked her, "But I can give you one 1,000Ft bill for a piece of bread."

The woman with the bread on the other side of the wire, said, "I don't care about the denomination of the bill, I just want three bills. They can be 500Ft or 1,000Ft or even a 5Ft. I just need three bills in exchange for this bread."

Flummoxed, the Hungarian woman asked her, "Why are you so caught up in the number of bills?" (I knew where this was going)

The woman on the other side of the fence who had the bread said, "I am out of toilet paper. I can tear up each bill into three parts and that will allow me nine wipes for this piece of bread."

The Hungarian woman was completely stupefied, "Why would you tear up money that you can spend?"

The woman replied, "Look around sister, money is not good here and we may not ever get out to spend it. What I need is toilet paper!" (With that, the exchange was made).

The Hungarian woman looked down at the rest of her bills, shook her head, and hid the remainder in her clothing. It is proven that money can't buy love. In here, it can't buy bread either by its value, but it can barter you toilet paper by its content.

Yours, Anne M. Frank

Saturday, December 16, 1944

My darling Kitty,

A strange occurrence I believe is happening here among us. I think love is blooming in the most unexpected place – Bergen-Belsen. It defies logic. There is no way this should be happening. We are sickly, weak, and emaciated. Our hair is growing out a little only because there are so many of us to cut. We don't smell good. Our clothes are dungy. We don't get to brush our teeth, which means we have bad breath. No one notices it anymore. Just as smokers don't smell smoke on other smokers, we don't notice the stench of each other.

How can there be love on our side of the fence? We are all women in our section, right? Right and wrong. There are only women in our part of the camp, but there are male guards. Kitty, you ask, "How can there be love? You mean between a prisoner and a guard?" I know it is conceivable that, in a warped way, a lady captive could fall in love with her captor, but that's not love if one loves and is not loved in return. What I am telling you is that there seems to be a love relationship blooming that is mutual. You say, "But guards bathe, are in clean uniforms, brush their teeth, and comb their hair, per Nazi regulations." That's right, they do.

"Then wouldn't a guard notice these women are unkempt even if it isn't their fault? Wouldn't they be afraid of disease? Wouldn't they notice the smell?" My answers to your questions are, "Yes. Yes. And, yes." So how?

I want to let you think about it for a while. How could this happen? Is it a guard for a Jewish girl? That alone is unnatural to the Nazi mindset. Is it Jewish girl for Jewish or non-Jewish girl? That would be unnatural, though I have shared with you some inclinations I have had in the past. These were due more to curiosity than anything else as a young girl facing puberty. So, what is it you ask? Who is it? I am going to let you have the night to think on it. This is just too good to drop on you all at once. The suspense should eat at you for a night. I spend my whole life in suspense Kitty. It won't hurt you to have a little in your life too.

Lovingly yours, Anne

Sunday, December 17, 1944

Dearest Kitty,

It was a long day today. Let me tell you all that we did....

You don't want to know that, do you? You want to know where is love in this camp. Okay, I am going to let the cat out of the bag, or at least the cat I think that is in the bag. Margot. Stop there.

Margot has been breaking away from me during and after our duties. We each need our space, being all cooped up together. I give her that space. I need mine too. She said she wanted to walk and exercise a little. It was no problem with me. One day, I let her go, went back to the barrack, but then got stir-crazy and took a walk myself. It was cold outside, but it was musty, dusty, and stank inside. I wrapped up in our blanket and took my walk. As I rounded the corner four barracks down from ours, I saw a guard facing someone leaning against the fifth barrack. I could tell it was a guard and it was an inmate girl. I got closer and knew from his hunched posture it was Izzo. Remember him, "Is so" mean? He had been gone for a few weeks. We figured to the war when he returned with a patch over his eye and a cast on his arm. I walked closer, trying not to stare, looking away as I took a circuitous route around them. They weren't hugging or anything, just in a serious conversation. I took one quick look as the girl covered her face. It was Margot! She was talking to Izzo as one would talk to a friend. I was dumbfounded! You think you know someone!

She returned to our barrack about an hour later. She just went about her business. I asked her, "How was your walk?" She said, "Fine." I asked her, "Is there anything you would like to tell me?" She said, "No, nothing." I said, "Well alright. You know I am your sister. You can tell me anything.." She said, 'I know."

What I wouldn't give to know what is going on there! I will give her time. In suffering, it is good to have someone other than family to talk to. I found that in Peter in the Annexe. Margot had no one. Now, we are in the camp. I don't have anyone to speak to other than imaginary friends, but if she has found someone, good for her. But Izzo?!!! A Nazi guard? I will give her a little space. Very little.

Yours, Anne M. Frank

Wednesday, December 20, 1944

My dearest Kit,

I finally got Margot to open up. How do you ask? I just point blank asked her, "Do you and Izzo have something going on?" Margot smiled her weak little smile. She said that he had asked her how she was doing a few days back. She told him she was doing as good as one could in a prison camp. He was apologetic, she said. He asked about where she was from, did she have family, other than me. He asked her where we were from and how we got here. She said she asked him similar questions. It turned out, he was forced into service after being in the Hitlerjugend, the Hitler Youth pipeline. He had seen action in the war, was injured, and sent to work in the camps to replace other able-bodied men sent to the front. He had believed in Hitler and all he was about, as did his family. They had been inebriated by the rhetoric. The more he got into it, the more disillusioned he became. He tried to get out because of his battle injuries, but they said the homeland needed him. He tried to use the terminal illness of his mother, but they would not give him a deferment. His dad died in North Africa. His brother died near Stalingrad. He was wounded in Normandy. His mother died due to neglect as there are no medical resources set aside for the elderly in need.

He confided in Margot that Germany was just a pile of rubble and all know that the end is near. He and his friends that he can trust, all hope that the generals will rise up and remove Hitler. Unfortunately, Hitler still has the Gestapo and his microphone, so it is hard to gain any traction. Besides that, the bad news is not reported. What the Germans know is just what they see firsthand, but wherever they are, they are told the devastation around them is the exception to the glorious victories the Fatherland is experiencing everywhere else. Long story short, Izzo tells Margot the war has to be coming to an end soon, but he wonders what will become of him now. He walks among the dead and the near-dead in this camp. Other than somewhat adequate diet and clean clothes to wear, there is no difference between the captives and the captors (Or so he says).

Margot asked him what he sees when he looks at her. She knows full well what she looks like. No mirror can lie unless there is one from a carnival. His answer? He told her he sees a woman destitute, scared, alone, worried, hungry, and starving. He was totally honest. He also said,

"Beneath your weather-beaten and abused appearance, I see beauty, love, and goodness. I see someone much better than I am." That was beautiful considering it came from a German Nazi soldier who holds a gun on us while he visits. I told Margot this. She is very sober about it all. She knows he would kill her if she were to try to run. He knows that duty demands it. He did say he would get us food if he could, but provisions are getting hard-to-come-by, even among the soldiers. The threat of desertion is so strong in their ranks that the gunfire heard outside the fence at night often isn't war. The gunshots are firing squads killing soldiers for the least bit of disobedience. Izzo told her that one soldier would kill another in a split-second if it meant more leniency for his family. He says the brutality has inflicted the Jew and the German alike.

Meanwhile, Hitler has his tea in his luxurious Eagle's Nest. He is driving the jeep of Germany over the cliff, and people are wiping his brow while he drives. The ignorance of it all is stupefying.

My opinion of Izzo? I don't trust him. He could be trying to get to Margot, to find out things we may be plotting inside the camp. He may be trying to cozy up to a prisoner to parlay any intel to his superiors, securing a higher rank. If that is not the case, then I still don't respect him. If he loves Margot or admires her, he ought to be getting her some food, which would get me some food too. No one who is decent, who opens up about their feelings, would be so cold and self-preserving to deny a fond friend. Love may be in the air, but I don't like its smell. I hope Margot sees it for what it is. She is pretty, smart, and wise. If it goes further, I pray that it will benefit all of us. I wish Mother were here. I think she would have plenty to say about this, as she did so many times before.

Yours, Anne M. Frank

Thursday, December 21, 1944

My dearest Kitty,

Margot is getting very defensive about her Nazi lover Izzo. She is not defensive about the Nazis, nor the SS, nor the Gestapo, nor the camps we are in, nor about the suffering we have experienced. She is just defensive regarding Izzo. She obviously doesn't remember him being "Is so" mean. I won't forget that he knocked me down several weeks ago. I won't forget that he ordered me to the infirmary or the pit, and that he didn't care which. I reminded Margot of this. Her answer, "He's just so scared!" My answer, "Let him spend the night in our barracks (not with you) and under the heavy hand of the superior race. Then we can visit about him being scared."

She told me about his family. She began it this way:

"Imagine for a moment that I am talking about a man named Franz, and that he is from Bulgaria. I tell you about how his family were strong Christians. They were in Church every day. They did business with the Jewish merchants and were always included in each other's religious holidays. Imagine I tell you that they had no idea what had happened to the Jewish neighbors, but before they could find out, they were caught up in a war. Like any person who loves his country and heritage, he went to fight for Bulgaria. He cared for the sick. He helped the dying. He risked his life for others. He cared for his mother and father by sending them letters and his military pay.

Imagine I tell you that before long, they realize their officers above them are doing unethical, inhumane things while they sleep. Later they find out that the enemies they were firing on were actually innocent women and children. When he found out, he tried to leave but they forced him to stay. What would you think then?"

I told her she writes a good story and that's all that is – a story. I was so mad. "You actually think these men are all doing this to us because they are misled and ignorant to what they are doing? If the Germans lose the war, and it seems they will, this would make one marvelous defense for their war crimes. I am not fooled for a moment. I know you have become cozy with one of our oppressors. And I know like Gisela from Auschwitz, each has a story of oppression and hardship. But, know this, if Izzo is on the up and up, he is an infinitesimal minority." I got lightheaded in my argument. A lack of food carried out by a guard named Izzo will do that to you. I laid down Kitty, wondering what is going on with my sister. One guy turns her head by giving her attention. Be he man or beast, she falls for him. How love hungry can she be? I wanted to question myself about Peter Van Daan, but I would not let that happen. This isn't about me. It's about Margot.

Rest easy, Kitty. Margot did return to her right mind. She and I agreed fully on the subject and I knew that she was not patronizing me. She and I have both lost everything. We agreed in no uncertain terms – there are hate crimes being carried out by every man who wears that swastika, and every one of them is guilty. They are without excuse. They could take a stand and give their lives for what is right. The fact that they don't makes them complicit. If they were truly sorry or regretful, life doesn't have enough hold to keep a true man from giving his very last drop of blood to correct an injustice. Pim did. We would. We are just women, sisters, and Jewish girls. We are desperate. We face death every day. We could easily kill the woman in our bunk for her bread. When we were in better physical shape, we could have had sex with a guard for an extra ration. We could have turned on Miep and Bep who helped us, if it would keep us at Westerbork. We did none of the above. We would rather give our lives than to do something so vicious and wrong. I imagine some of those gunshots in the distance at night are for German men who stood up against these Nazi demonic acts. I told Margot, "You'll notice, Izzo is still here. What does that tell you?"

Yours, Anne M. Frank

Friday, December 22, 1944

Dearest Kitty,

Yesterday evening's conversation must have hit its mark with Margot. She did not take a walk without me. We saw Izzo down the aisle of barracks. He smiled. Margot grabbed my arm and we went in a different direction. Later, he came to the barrack to "check to see that all were in compliance with camp rules." His goal was actually to check on Margot. He inspected our quarters, rifled through all the residents' belongings, lifted our blankets as if looking for hidden goods, made some housecleaning demands, growled, and left our habitation. Later, we found a piece of bread under our blanket. I wonder. Was this the mysterious donor?

It didn't matter, and what I am about to tell you Kitty will shock you. Neither of us ate the bread. Margot took it to him at twilight. She said she handed it to him and told him that if he were really against what we were facing, she expected him to be a man and take his stand. She could not respect him or talk to him otherwise. She reminded him of Pim and all he had done for us, the family he loved.

How did Izzo take it? Margot said, "We'll see, but I would not get my hopes up. He snatched the bread from my hand, told me to leave his sight, and then he stormed away." My answer to Margot, "Great, as if things could not get any worse for us! Thanks Margot!." She nudged me in the ribs with her bony elbow and smiled. We are sisters for sure.

Yours, Anne M. Frank

Saturday, December 23, 1944

Dearest Kitty,

Another day. The longer we are here, the more I fear that all our dreams are no longer in reach. We get weaker and sicker by the day. Margot was so tough yesterday with Izzo. Now, I think she has break-up remorse. For a short time there, she had me and another to distract her from our torment. She was tasting love like I had tasted with Peter. The question she was struggling with was, "Did I miss my only chance for love? Was he Mr. Right and I let him go?" I think every person who has ever loved and lost feels this way. We walk through life thinking there is only one love that God has for us, that we can toy with it, like a fish on a hook, knowing that it will always be there to reel in when we are ready. We are then shocked when the fish gets off the hook. We sit there looking at the line, waiting for another bite. The worm is gone. The hook no longer has its lure.

I think Margot and I both look at each other in our condition and wonder if we have lost our lure? Who would have us in this state? There is no beauty in what we see in ourselves. The very fact that a man could be drawn to Margot here in the starvation capital of the world is a shock. That a well-fed guard with a life beyond these fences could ever find attraction inside the gated area defies logic. Of all the frauleins available to him, of all the families he could marry into, it is clear this relationship was doomed from the start. I am sure this is Margot's logic. It would be mine.

I believe the argument, though, is made from desperation and depression. I don't believe there is just that one person out there, and if you miss him, you missed your one chance for love. There has to be love beyond the one. Courting is always the act of finding the right fit. Peter and I courted. I saw in him many attributes that I felt would make him a great match for me. He was brave. He was cute. He was humble. He was boyish, which for some reason appeals to us girls. He was my opposite. At the time, that seemed to be a negative. Now looking at Father and Mother, I see that is perhaps the Divine Plan. Later, I realized that there could be a better fit for me than Peter. I wanted someone who would not be so dependent upon me. Could I have made it with Peter? Yes. Could I have made it with Peter Schiff? I think so. Could I have made it a go with Hello? Yes. He was one of my closest friends. Who better to marry than a friend, who knows you going into the nuptials?

Is there another man for me? Is there another man for Margot? I believe so, if we ever get out of here. Arranged marriages seem to work well. The boy didn't choose the girl. The girl didn't choose the boy. The parents chose the arrangement. Somehow, they make it work. They grow to love each other often because love is a commitment and not an emotion alone. When left to their own choices, they might have ended up together, or they might not have. Marriage is what you make of it. Marriage is a decision. You determine that you will spend your life with this person or that person. Father and Mother made that decision and married on Pim's birthday. They traveled to Italy for their honeymoon, and then stepped forward to live their lives together. They had two beautiful and highly gifted daughters. I had to add that truth to the result!

I am sure there were days that Father wished to be with someone else. I know there were days I wished he had been with someone else. I know in Mother's complaining, she probably felt she could have found someone more suited to her taste. I know that no one is a better man than Father. If she had found someone else, she would not have been as happy. I think of Mrs. Van Daan and all her flirting. She flirted with Father. She flirted with Dussel. She is here now and tries to flirt with certain guards. She thinks she still is attractive. I have never seen her grieve over her separation from Mr. Van Daan. Mother grieved constantly for Father and kept his memory in many of our conversations at Auschwitz.

I remind Margot of all this. It seems to be a one-sided conversation. She doesn't respond much, but I think I am getting my point across. I feel that we should not settle for an Izzo just because we are desperate to be loved, or fret that our opportunity will pass us by. We should not just marry whoever is willing because we are lonely. I contend that it is better to be alone and lonely than to be married and miserable. Forgive me, Kitty, for sounding like I am taking both sides of the argument. Let me sum up my discussion. Thank you for letting me because as I work it out with you, I can reason with Margot better. I believe we can find love and marriage in more than one candidate. I also believe there can be a wrong candidate. Margot should not grieve over the break-up with Izzo thinking there will be no other men. Margot should also not try to resume ties with Izzo because the wrong mate is worse than no mate.

Confusingly Yours, Anne M. Frank

Sunday, December 24, 1944

Dearest Kitty,

One minute, I am the queen of philosophy, and the next minute I am in the depths of depression. Margot feels the same. We finished our work today and were denied any bread for the umpteenth time. It may be because they have too many of us Jews to feed, or it may be because Izzo is getting back at us. Either way, it is Christmas Eve. It is so easy to look at what we once had, see what we no longer have, and wonder if there can

ever be happiness again. Many here are dwelling on this fact. Hanukkah,
St. Nicholas' Day, and Christmas are the happiest days of the year, as are
birthdays. That is in theory, because here at Bergen-Belsen, as in Auschwitz, they are the most depressing.

It's sad to know there are gifts being given, songs being sung, food
being eaten, and families being gathered. That is forbidden for any of us
here. The more we think about it, the more it bothers us. We do a lot of
listening around here to the guards. We hope to hear what is going on in
the war. We hope to catch what might become of us. We try to gain insight into any food that might be ours if we can catch a clue where food
might be. Of late, the guards are talking out loud about what they are
doing tonight after their shift, and tomorrow if they are off work. These
holidays make them even meaner to us. They blame us for taking them
from their families. Many are crueler during this season because they
hate us so much. I think this is why they almost braggingly tell what they
will eat, what they will drink, how they will sing and celebrate, while we
stay in our dark, cold barracks, starving and dying of sickness. How cruel
can they be?

Margot is not feeling well today. I don't think it is love-sickness. She
has a fever. She also is very down. After her display a while back in the
infirmary, I am very sensitive that she does not lose her wits. She was
taking me down the road of despair when I remembered what Pim used
to do when we were sad. He would recall some happy memory and get
us talking about it. Other times, he would talk about some future event
that we were looking forward to. Father just wanted to get our minds off
the subject. So, I said to Margot, "Remember the time that Father and
Mother took us to see Shirley Temple in the movie 'Heidi'?" Margot
smiled. She and I both loved Shirley Temple movies. She reminded me
of the plot of that movie and how it compared to ours. In that movie,
Shirley Temple plays the role of Heidi, who is taken from her home and
forced to work for a wealthy man caring for the man's daughter. Heidi

takes the job as a young girl and loves the little lady she is caring for, but begins to long to go back home. She thinks that one day she will be able to go home and decides to make the best of the situation. However, soon she finds that the girl's family has no intention of ever letting her go. Thankfully, it all works out in the end. I told Margot that I had forgotten that; but of course, I was pretty young then.

We laughed about our family times together with Father and Mother. Harkening back to the movie 'Heidi', I said, "We feel like we will never get out of here; that the Germans won't let us go. We had hoped this would all end soon, but it hasn't. Still Margot, I believe this will end well." Margot answered, "I sure hope you're right Anne. I sure hope you're right." I nodded my head, "Me too."

We were headed to another stage of sadness, and I reminded her of the movies Father would bring home after the curfews were placed on us. We loved Rin Tin Tin, especially the movie, "The Lighthouse by the Sea." What a glorious story that was. Margot and I both remembered this one. We talked about the plot of the man in the lighthouse going blind and how the daughter had to run it for him, so that he could keep his job. What a courageous girl that was. Margot said that she is trying to be that brave little girl here. Father and Mother are helpless, but we can carry on and hopefully one day take care of our parents too. I loved that. Margot was starting to shake-off her depression. She talked about the bad guys the girl in the movie had to encounter and how with the help of a man and his dog, they were able to push back the bad guys. I told her that maybe one of these guards with his dog will help us. I also told her that it would not be Izzo. He doesn't have a dog!

Yours, Anne M. Frank

Monday, December 25, 1944

My dearest Kit,

Merry Christmas! We had felt sad, but one of the ladies in our bar-racks who has an amazing voice began to sing Christmas carols. It was simply Heaven-sent. She stood by the fence that separated two sections of our camp, the one that has food and the one that doesn't. She began to sing, and so many of us joined her. There are so many nationalities here. Most don't speak all the languages we do, having never had the oppor-tunity to learn as we did. That did not matter. The tune was the same, the lyrics were too, but sung in different languages. It was one of the most beautiful things we had ever experienced. The guards, who were on duty in the towers were lenient. I think they wanted a little home themselves. Friend or enemy, one has to appreciate God-given talent. This woman, I believe her name was Caroline, just graced us with song. We would sing, but sometimes there would be a shush go across the yard. No one was trying to stop the singing, but people just wanted to hear her sing some songs alone.

It reminded me of the days that we would sit in the alley near the concert venue in our town. The concert would be sold-out, but Pim and others would sit outside because we could still enjoy the glory of song without having to pay a penny for it. They could keep us out, but they could not keep the music in. I think there is a lesson there, Kitty. I sat on that cold hard ground with Margot, with our blanket covering our shoul-ders, and we were listening to this wonder of music here in the ugliest place on earth. What a Christmas gift! It was real. It could not be wasted. It could not be hoarded. It could only be shared. No one had to reach for it. The sick and the well could equally benefit from it. There was no charge. An unexplainable oneness permeated the camp. I looked up as we sang 'Silent Night', and I saw the guards leaning over from the towers singing too. Tears filled my eyes. Why must there be hate and war? The captors and the captives can come together. We are humans, all of us, even when some act inhumane. We hurt. We love. We sacrifice. We need. We long. We dream. We want.

What was it that was bringing us together? It was Christmas. The natural question is, what is it about Christmas that can do this? The Christians celebrate Christmas, the birth of Jesus. Miep and Bep, Kugler and Kleiman, all celebrated Christmas. We had met no people more wonderful and caring. They were willing to risk their lives for us. That is what they said Jesus did too. Miep told me that Jesus brought hope into the world, and that His disciples called Him the Prince of Peace. That resonated with me. One of our favorite verses concerning the Messiah was found in Isaiah, chapter nine. I remembered this one from our studies of our nation's prophets because I just thought it was so beautiful and poetic, "For unto us a child is born, unto us a son is given, and the government will be on his shoulders. And he will be called Wonderful Counselor, Mighty God, Everlasting Father, Prince of Peace." As we sang for hours on end, this Christmas holiday was about what peace could look like. Christmas was about a child being born, about a son being given, and about a prince of peace. I am not sure what all this means. I know what Miep told me it meant. I wondered if this was why Father wanted to expand my knowledge to the New Testament a few Christmases ago.

We sang. Some songs we knew. Some we learned. We wanted to learn them; to sing them in our language. A symphony is made up of many instruments playing together. Our singing was a symphony of different languages singing together. A light snow began to fall. We saw purity. We saw white. We saw each individual snowflake that fell, and as our heads were lifted up, the wet drops landed on our ears, noses, foreheads, and cheeks. Yet, none of us felt cold. "Merry Christmas to all, and to all a good night."

Yours, Annelies Marie Frank

Tuesday, December 26, 1944

My dearest Kitty,

The shift of guards was changed today, and so was the mood in the camp. I wish last night's guards could have stayed on through the rest of the war. They had experienced something last night. We all had. This makes me more perturbed at men like Izzo. They see what peace is. They realize we are humans, no less than they. We have no wicked intent. They can see that. Why can't they see that this is not true on their side. Why can't they take last night of Christmas wonder and use it as an agent of change? I wish they would report to their commanders what they experienced on Christmas. Maybe some of them did. Quite possibly, the ones who had the courage to do so are now headed to the front to fight the Russians or to the firing squads tonight outside the fence.

Fear overwhelms everyone in this war. Perhaps Hitler, Himmler, Goebbels, and Mengele are the only ones with no fear because they are too demon-possessed to care. I don't understand why no one stands up to them. Where are the German people? I know there are some great Germans out there. My Father and Mother were born German, and grew up German. They were German until the Nazis started dividing German from Jew. Our parents did business with Germans. They socialized with Germans. They helped their fellow-Germans. They knew Germans who helped others. Surely, they can't be the minority.

This morning, after a glorious yesterday, there was more work, less rations, and more dead bodies in our barracks. I envy those who died before morning. At least, they died happy and with hope. Hope is taking a beating today. Our outlook isn't so good. I wonder if we have reached a point of no turning back. After D-Day, I had begun to pay attention to Father's map on the wall in the Annexe tracking the progress of the Allied invasion, as well as the ebb and flow of the war. This map gave us hope. I would ask Miep all the time what the news was. Her report would give us hope while we lived in the shadow of darkness. The Annexe seemed like darkness, but we were just on the edge of it. After our arrests and the trip to Auschwitz, we were plunged into total darkness. No news cripples our hopes. We are listening more to our guards. We are trying to read their moods and facial expressions. We are noting their movements in and out of camp and their various policy changes here. This is now our hope. What we gain from the circumstantial indicators is our only insight to the happenings outside. What we perceive is good news. What we fear is that we perceive what we want to perceive instead of what is. We constantly think that it won't be long. Those who believe the instruments on the dial are inaccurate are often carried outside the barrack, to be thrown into the pit soon after.

Yours, Anne M. Frank

Wednesday, December 27, 1944

Dearest Kitty,

When I was young, Father and Mother decided to take us on a trip to see Grandma. I wanted to look my best, so I packed my bags and was ready to go. Mother looked at my hair and asked me if I was going to go with my hair looking the way it did. Because I loved my hair and how it looked, I raced to the sink and washed it. Before I could get it dry and styled, Father said we had to go. My hair was wet as we stepped into the cold air on our way to the train station. It was the funniest thing. I felt fine one minute, but the next minute, I could almost tell you the exact moment it happened, I felt sick. A head cold came over me. I had a fever. I had chills. I went hoarse and could hardly speak. What shocked me was the realization of how quickly sickness can come upon you.

You can be well and gradually get sick. You can also be well and with the snap of your fingers, you are sick instantaneously. Why do I tell you this? Because we woke up this morning and I was feeling fine. I stepped out into the cold. My head was still damp, I suppose, from nighttime sweats. Now I am sick and nauseated – me and thousands all around me. I pray this is just a passing thing. There is no chicken soup here for the sick, no pampering, no taking my temperature, no wet towel on my forehead, no books brought to my bedside while I recover, and no kiss on the cheek. What do they do when we get sick? They scream at us, "Get out of bed you lazy, good-for-nothing!" Of course, if we are good-for-nothing, why not leave us in bed? If we are that much of a waste, why not kill us all and go home? I still wrestle with the question of why are we here.

I am thankful for Margot. She cares for me. She watches out for me and I watch out for her. It seems more and more that this life is going to be shared by just she and I. I am so glad she is here. She reminds me more and more of Father, but with the marvelous Margot-flavor.

Yours, Anne M. Frank

Thursday, December 28, 1944

Dearest Kitty,

Now Margot feels she is starting to come down with something. She got me tucked in and brought me a piece of bread that she had lifted from somewhere. She then laid down beside me. I heard her say something that I had never heard her say before:

As we lay quietly, she said, 'This is all my fault."

I rolled over and looked at her, "Why would you say that? How is this your fault?" It wasn't her fault I was sick. It wasn't her fault that I caught a cold. I asked her, "What is your fault?"

She said, "If only Father would have let me answer that summons to go to the Nazi work camp July 5, 1942, maybe none of this would be happening. You and the rest of our family would be safe in Switzerland by now. It seems like such a waste to put the whole family at risk for one daughter. Isn't it better that one suffers and perhaps dies than all of us? A lot of families faced the same dilemma we faced back then, Anne. They hated it, but they let their child go off to work camp. This bought the family time to decide what they needed to do. If only I would have been more courageous. If only I would have demanded that Father let me go, or if I would have just run out and removed the choice from him. Who knows, maybe I would be in a better place now. You, Father, and Mother would be too."

I could not believe my ears. I said, "Margot Bettie Frank, this thought had never entered my mind, nor Father's or Mother's. We have been in this together from the beginning. We left Frankfurt together. We moved into the Annexe together. We were in Auschwitz together. Though we are apart from Father and Mother, we are in this trial together. By God's Grace, we will get out of this together. If it had been my name called, you would have wanted us to hide and protect me. If Father's name had been called, you would have been the first to pack his bag and ours. I love you. I know I have seldom ever said those words, but you know they are true. I cannot believe what I am about to say, but here it goes. I would rather be here with you, than to have you here going through this and me be in some other place."

Margot said, "That's sweet of you to say, Anne, but..."

"No buts about it Margot", I interrupted. "Once again, you remind me of Father. If he could go through all this for us, he would. You are the same. A few years ago, I don't think I could have said what I just said to you. I think when I was younger and less mature, I would gladly let Mother take this for us or you rather than us."

Margot, in her tears, giggled, "I know you would have let us too!"

I was not offended, "You are right. Isn't it interesting how the fire boils out the impurities. We are in the fire, and I feel many of my impurities and faults are being purged. I really do want us to get out of here. I believe we will be beautiful to behold on the other end of this and we can make a lasting difference on the world around us."

Margot concurred, "May it be, Anne."

I joked back, "Now, if only you could get a summons out of here back to our homes. I know that me, Father, and Mother would love to pack up and move with you. Can you do something about that, big sister?"

Margot: "I will try my best!"

And she kissed me on the cheek. I hugged her. What a blessing. If we have to be in the fire, I want us together.

Yours, Anne M. Frank

Friday, December 29, 1944

Dearest Kitty,

I wish you could go back and check on our apartment in Amsterdam. I would love to know if any of our neighbors are left. We saw many through our Annexe window being marched out. The thought we have here is that no one has survived. As far as we know, the only survivors are those who are in this camp. Each day, those we know have succumbed to the barbarous acts of deprivation. Just as we imagine most of our friends are gone, we fear greatly so are our parents. I just can't see Father making it past the first selection. Age would prohibit it per the Mengele mind. Mother? I don't think she could make it without us. We refuse to speculate because that would only cause us to want to let go. We do know Anne is alive as is Margot. I wonder if Mother and Father are alive and think we are dead. They probably have better hope for us than we do for them. The minute the train pulled out of Auschwitz, there was a relief that perhaps now we would have a chance. If only they could see this place. I am not sure they would be so positive if they saw this place. In Auschwitz, death is forced. Here, death is voluntary. Though it is a decision of the will, more and more are willful to leave this place via the pit.

How many of our friends are gone? How many of our friends are alive thinking we are gone. "Poor Anne, she was so young and frail. There is no way she would make it through this. Margot, maybe, but Anne? No way." I just know that is the thought. When we went to Westerbork, Father tried to get me a better work detail because he was not sure I could take the rigors of the battery detail and the dust. Pim was sweet to try, but I was stronger than he thought. I have a will to live; to push through to survive. That will subside at times, but it catches its breath and jumps back up within me. Margot is showing a surprisingly strong will herself. She was so passive growing up. Deep down, she has to have had a conversation with herself about what she would do. I am so proud of her. I know Father would be proud of both of us.

Kitty, I never wanted you to share my letters with others, but I wish now you could share this letter to let all know the Frank sisters survive.

We are bent but not broken. If you were able to do that, please also tell them to hurry up. We need some relief here!

Yours, Anne M. Frank

Sunday, December 31, 1944

My dearest Kitty,

The new year is upon us. At the stroke of midnight, I would like to say, "Happy New Year!", but will it be? In our Jewish religion, it is comparable to Rosh Hashanah, though the Jewish calendar doesn't coincide with the rest of the world's. In our native faith, it is a time to blow the trumpets and celebrate change from the bad or a continuation of the good. In this case, we want a change from the bad. The soldiers have started drinking early. You would think it was Hitler's birthday again. We would celebrate for a cool drink of clean, fresh water. They eat delicacies. We just want to eat. They hope for victory. We hope for their defeat. They think their victory will bring on a thousand-year reign. We know that only in their defeat will justice ever reign. How alike we were at Christmas here in the camp, and how different we are one month later at New Year's.

I pray on this day that God will move on our behalf. I pray to see the world change for good. I pray the Nazi machine will be cut down and never be allowed to rise in any corner of the world. I pray that all people can live together in harmony and peace. I pray that we will be set free. I can't imagine how we can get our lives back, but getting out is the only way to start that process. I pray that Mother and Father are both alive. God gives life. God takes life. We learned from Elisha that God can give life back to those who are dead. We learned in Ezekiel that God can raise up dry bones, and give them flesh, meat, organs, and breath. I pray God will raise up, heal, and breathe on these bones of ours that have no meat, but only infested flesh with deflating breath.

New Year's is a time of hope. It is a time to turn the calendar over. We cannot revisit the past. I do not wish to revisit the last two and half years. There is a new year coming, 1945. May this be the year, early in the year, that our dreams come true. I once dreamed to go to Hollywood or Paris, and to be known. Now, I just dream of being free. We are going to bed, weary and sick. We have no watches, but I am sure it is well before midnight. I feel we have been living at midnight for far too long.

The guns were fired, waking us from our deep sleep. I was dreaming I was with Peter in the attic. I was enjoying my time, at least in my mind, of not being here. The gunfire brought me back to Bergen-Belsen. There was cheering from the soldiers. I hope that is the cheering for the New Year and not for some news of their victory over the forces of good.

Yours, Anne M. Frank

Monday, January 1, 1945

Dearest Kitty,

The turn of the calendar made no difference. We are still here, still sick, and still hungry. People are still dying. We had seven dead in our barrack this morning. For them, it is a new year of freedom. For the rest of us, we have to help carry them out of our front door. Before we do that, we take their blankets and any clothing or shoes that are better than our own. We search the spot where they had lain for any food they had squirreled away. It is hard to be moved by someone's death anymore. It is a daily experience. We wake up and count the dead. Or, we don't wake up and are counted as dead.

We itch and we scratch. Sores come from the thin skin we have. With that scratch, comes infection and swelling. I am fifteen years old, but I look now much older. I am a woman, but in my frailty, I have no shape or curves. My beautiful hair is now matted and thin. When it does grow, it grows in brittle and fragile. There are bugs in our beds and bugs in our hair. There are still fleas and lice. At least in Auschwitz, they fought the lice. Here, it is as if Bergen has surrendered the camp to lice. In Auschwitz, they fought the contagion. Here, they feed it. We are growing sicker.

Margot could not go to the fence this evening, but I did go hoping for some bread to be thrown over the fence. I was not successful as many days past. Why keep going to the fence if we return with nothing? It seems like a waste of limited energy. We go because no bread is being thrown into our barracks. You can't get bread lying in the bed. You have to go and get it. There is no room service, no bed-side delivery. We cannot live on what the SS feeds us. Just as one should work to feed one's family, we work for food. The work we do for the Nazis is not to get something but to avoid something – pain and injury. Our work for food comes after our work for the Nazi. Initiative, resourcefulness, and the kindness of strangers in similar states is our only provision for life.

I am about to sleep now, Kitty. I pray that the powers-that-be allow the Red Cross to give us packages, too. I don't know why the Red Cross won't insist on it. Maybe they are told to be happy with who gets them. The guards could stop that if they wanted. How hard and callous the Nazis are.

Yours, Anne M. Frank

Thursday, January 4, 1945

Dearest Kitty,

I am too weak to think. I am having a hard time keeping up with the days. I try to count the sunrises and mark them from the date I do know – Monday, January 1, 1945. I wonder if we have reached the point of no return now. I feel like we have been walking to get to the foot of the rainbow just to have that foot constantly moving kilometers ahead of us. We focus our eyes on where the rainbow touches the ground. We note the markers around it. We get to that very place. Even though the rainbow is moved, the spot is certain. We look down. There is no pot of gold, but just a pot of cold and empty.

From what I see in so many here, there is a point where death is certain. There is no hope at that stage for healing, even if a true doctor were to show up with the equipment and medicine to cure. I fear that even if the Allies do show up in a few days, most of us would still die. Let the Nazis flee and the gates be permanently opened. Bring us food and water, blankets, and warmth, and we would still die. Why? Because we have reached the point of no return. I look at Margot's face and body. I feel she is close to that. She doesn't talk to me much anymore. She looks into space. She nods her head. That is the only way I know she hears me. She is distraught and I fear she has given up.

Margot once was my older sister, who was taller, healthier, more athletic, engaged, and curvy. I have passed her up, but not by much. I am taller because she slumps. I am healthier because I can get out of bed. I am more athletic because I can make it to the fence. I am engaged because I can still carry on a cogent conversation. I am not curvy though. Lay me down beside her undressed and cover our faces. You will see there is no difference in our bodies at all. What is the difference? Will, I suppose. Maybe it's not will. Maybe it is just that I have not reached the quitting point just yet. It's not that I won't quit. It is just I'm not ready to quit yet. I see a finish line. I am exhausted, but seeing the finish line makes me want to lean into the tape and then collapse. That is such a false illustration. I see no finish line. At least, I see no finish line for victory. If death is a finish line for us, it won't be a "Our run has been victorious" finish line, but rather a "Our run is complete and over" finish line.

My run is not complete, but I am rounding the homestretch. Margot must be a little ahead of me, as she has always been. I do not want to run this race without my sister. I have always run behind her. I have always looked at her back and tried to keep pace. When she could ride the bike next to Father, and I was in the stroller with Mother, I wanted to be on that bike. When she was studying at higher levels, I wanted to study what she studied. The adults in the Annexe used to say some books of Margot's were too old for me. I wanted to hurry up and get to the point where I could read them too. Margot has given me a reason to live, and a reason to reach, and a reason to strive. We are only three years apart. There is no reason she should go three years ahead of me. We are close enough in age that we should be able to finish the course together a long way down the line of years. I want that. Margot used to want that. I am not sure she cares anymore. I am pestering her though. You can bet on that!

Yours, Anne M. Frank

Saturday, January 6, 1945

Dearest Kitty,

You will never guess who came by to check on us – Mrs. Van Daan. She is not in our barrack at the moment, but she knew where we were. She has noticed that she is seeing me a lot more than Margot and had worried that maybe Margot had been carried out with the dead wood. How often do some of our camp busybodies walk in front of the barracks, looking over the dead to see if they recognize anyone? I don't grieve like I once did, but I also don't go to see who I have outlasted either.

That is not nice for me to say. I want the Good Anne to dominate my life, not the Bad Anne. It was nice of her to come and check on us. She even brought a piece of bread for us to share. I let Margot have it. I had to pretend that I took a bite, so Margot would eat the rest. I put the bread in my hand, my hand to my mouth, and I began to chew. I then handed the piece to Margot, pretending it was her half. It was only after she saw me chewing and a crumb just happened to stick to my face that she ate. I may have even fooled Mrs. Van Daan.

She has heard nothing of Mr. Van Daan or Peter. She does grieve for Peter and feels he is still alive and well. She says she asks new arrivals if they have seen her family or ours. She says sometimes the people tell her they have. We are used to this. No one really wants to give bad news. They will lie and say our loved ones are fine in the hopes that we will continue living with a purpose. However, we have caught on to this kind fabrication, and ask a few questions about our family. It is then that we catch them in their merciful deceit. Thankfully, our interrogation so far has just affirmed that they have not seen our loved ones. We have not received any hint that any new arrivals have seen the death of those we love so dear.

Mrs. Van Daan is holding up well. She looks bad, but she looks better than the rest of us. I would say "only the good die young," but again that would be Bad Anne talking. I don't know why I am so sarcastic. I really think it is because I am trying to be funny. I like to say obnoxious things even to you, Kitty, to relieve the pressure or to bring amusement. Though we are dying, it seems, I want to show my disdain for all of this. They can keep us out of the concert, but they cannot keep us from hearing the music. I still hear the music. I still feel life inside of me. I may look like a prisoner. I may truly be too weak to fight physically, but on the inside, I am fighting them. Mentally, I feel I am whipping them. I may not be able to cut them with whips, but I am cutting them with quips. Pim was the poet in the family. I am starting to get more of his rhyme though. That makes me smile. I shared this with Margot. She gave me a faint smile.

Yours, Anne M. Frank

Monday, January 8, 1945

Dearest Kitty,

We are still having roll call. Elizabeth and I (yes, she is still here in our bunk) helped Margot out and down. Our bunk is the second one up and right beside the frigid door. Heat does not seem to travel up in this place. We carry her to the roll call. In Auschwitz, they would have already selected Margot. I am glad we are not in Auschwitz. Once the headcount is through, we help her back to the bed. One holds her back, while the other lifts her legs. It is not that she is heavy. She is extremely light. It is just that we are as weak as she is light. It takes us both. Sometimes, Caroline the singer comes and helps us.

Caroline is weak too, but her voice is strong. Give her a swallow of water in the evening, and she gives us a song. Margot seems to really light up at the music. It is not Christmas anymore. The guards hate the song. Caroline's service to the campers is she goes from barrack to barrack (for those who ask) and sings one song. With that completed, she leaves and returns to her barrack. Her gift to us – a song that echoes in our minds. We sing it in our sleep. We may not have a good voice, but in our minds, we join in perfect pitch.

Yours, Anne M. Frank

Wednesday, January 10, 1945

My dearest Kitty,

I am working alone on the grounds. My job? I am to go around and see how many cracks there are in each barrack that are in-need-of-repair. It is so cold outside. There is no need for this nonsense. They are not going to repair these barracks unless German soldiers have to move in. They are trying to kill us, I think, but slowly. I had to sit down many times. Often, I would go into each barrack and check for cracks on the inside. This allowed me to sit down inside nearly every building I surveyed. I would go around the outside rather quickly, and then go to the inside where the wind was blocked. I felt safe doing this. If a guard questioned me, I would just tell them, "If you really want this job done, I must be thorough. A crack on the outside isn't too serious unless it has penetrated to the inside." That argument would win the day, as long as they don't see me laying in a barrack's bunk. I guess I could tell them I am checking the ceiling for cracks too!

After my work, I checked on Margot. She has rallied a bit. She got out of bed on her own, but is very weak still. She can walk a few steps, and then she has to sit down. She is a trooper. She gets up every so often. She says she must build up her strength or lose it completely.

I told her I was going to the fence to check for food. I did that and my prize was an old apple core. There were still some bites left on it, so I took it to Margot. We shared it. I then went back out after our prayers. I could not sleep. It was silent out. The darkness would hide me. The camp lay totally still and silent. It was as if no one was here. I walked in the shadows. There was not a sound. I closed my eyes and imagined the camp had been abandoned. Perhaps they have all been moved or liberated. It didn't matter. There was this feeling that I was visiting a historic place where once horrors were the main menu of each day.

I began to fantasize that I was a visitor to this place; a tourist coming to a place of memorial. I could see signs at the gate telling what the name of this place was. I saw guide signs at certain barracks, telling a story of a person who was kept there. I walked to the pit on the edge of camp and imagined what the plaque would say about the piles and piles of bodies that lay beneath this sod. I made my way to where the old infirmary was, now converted to just another barrack because everyone is sick. I pictured a historic plaque there telling of the rampant diseases that had hit this place and how poorly the sick were treated. I got to the corner of one of the barracks; the one closest to the guard tower. I hugged the corner of it to stay in the shadow. The guard was looking out into the field. I could tell because of the glow of his cigarette. I imagined a plaque below the tower telling of what hate-filled men once guarded this place. I walked to the gate where the transports and the marches of death-row inmates came. They weren't death-row by act, but death-row by omission. I could have written this plaque detailing the thousands who were brought here thinking this was a better place than the one they had just left. They would be greatly disappointed. I gradually made my way to the fence with the straw that separated those of us who have nothing from those of us who have next to nothing. This plaque would read how the Red Cross packages came and people with very little shared with those who had none. It would tell of how we stood here for hours praying that something would come over, or be handed underneath. I finally made my way to the inner corner of our section as it touches the others. I would conjecture a plaque here that told the numbers of the imprisoned and dead.

There was indeed silence. How sobering to think that mankind could do this to their own. I felt a pain in my side that then pinched down below. I sat in the silence, heard the wind gently blow, and smelled the moisture from the hills. The cold made a sharp cut through my loosely hanging clothes into my feeble hanger of a body. I am not a tourist here.

There are people still in this place suffering. This tragic story has not been fully written. I long for the final chapter.

Yours, Anne

Saturday, January 13, 1945

Dearest Kitty,

There is truly an epidemic that has hit us. For those of us able to get out of bed, we are overwhelmed by the lifeless bodies prone and uncovered outside each barrack. It is like a trash day in some cities where on a particular day, everyone puts their trash out to be picked up. Every day to the Nazi guards, it is trash day. Of course, they don't handle the dead as much as forcing others to do it. The body crews once could wait a few days until they hit their body limit and then they would make their run to the pit. That count is now reached every day, sometimes twice per day.

I stepped out this morning, as I seek to every morning. The smell on the inside is smothering. Because of that, the cold is refreshing. The freezing seems to reduce the smell or the sense of smell. I saw so many bodies being dragged out of our barrack. When I went out, I saw that the bodies were everywhere. Could it be typhus, as they say, or could they be poisoning us? For this many people to die all at once, you would think Mengele had come up with some new form of mass genocide. He didn't come up with it, but the form of imprisonment seems to have accomplished it just the same.

As I stepped out, I saw some of our fellow prisoners loading the mostly naked bodies into the wheelbarrow. Not all were naked because there are just too many to strip. It's not worth the effort anymore. We must conserve our energy. Besides, so many dead have really made it where everyone has had plenty of covers. Sadly, those covers are covered in lice and fleas. Who notices them anymore?

Anyway, I saw the body crew, three ladies, pushing the wheelbarrow. A guard was prompting them on. One of the women dropped. He checked her for life. Without saying a word, he had the other two put her in the wheelbarrow too. He called out to another prisoner to take her place. Off they went, absent of emotion, to the pit to make their dump.

Tuesday, January 16, 1945

My dearest Kitty,

Please do not think I am weary of you. I am just weary of thinking. If I were writing my letters to you again, I would have stopped writing long ago. No surplus of pens or paper can keep me writing when there is no strength left to do so. I don't think I am competent enough now to write a complete sentence or to edit my work. Now, I can't think very clearly. I am getting more confused as the days wear on.

Margot is sick again. We both have headaches, fever, and chills. I am still hungry and looking for food. I walk out, constantly bumping into people, or they bump into me. No one minds. We mechanically go through our routines. We are alive, but not living. The guards are tired too. They aren't even that regular with our roll calls, at least on this side of the fence. They are half-hearted. I don't think they fear escape anymore from any of us. We hardly have the strength to get up. We are not in running shape anymore. It is not all of us, but even those who feel well see little hope of staying that way. There is little talk in our barracks. Caroline isn't singing anymore.

Friday, January 19, 1945

My dearest Kitty,

Rachel is another lady in our barrack. She sleeps on the other end. I had not really visited with her before. With the sickness growing more rampant, some of the familiar faces are growing closer together. Rachel is half-Jewish, I believe. She is unclear about her heritage. It may be that she cannot remember it. Or, it may be that she has been telling that for so long, to get out of here, that now she believes it. I don't know any of that for certain. What I do know is that she is nice. She checks on Margot and me daily as she passes our bunk. She also helps me from time to time, to get Margot up.

I told her about Margot's study of religion and how she had hoped to one day go to Jerusalem to finish her education and to work. Rachel was intrigued. I told her I wanted to be a writer, but that desire is dulling with every passing day. Rachel told me that she wants to be a teacher of religion. She has studied the Old and New Testament. Her strength is memory. She was taught early on to stretch the mind, to read, memorize, and recite. She was always the first in her class in memorizing Scripture. I thought that was neat, but I wasn't sure if I believed her.

She really amazed me. I would tell her of some passage in Isaiah that I was familiar with. She would quote it whole-cloth. Margot was better at it than me. I asked Margot to give her a part of the Old Testament to quote. I then whispered in her ear, "Give her one that you know so that we can see if she is telling the truth." After all, if we don't know the Bible, how can we know she is not making it all up. We wouldn't know enough to tell the difference. Margot then said half-voice, half-whisper, in her weakened state, "Psalm 22." With that, Rachel went to town:

"Psalm 22. My God, my God, why hast thou forsaken me? why art thou so far from helping me, and from the words of my roaring? O my

God, I cry in the daytime, but thou hearest not; and in the night season, and am not silent. But thou art holy, O thou that inhabitest the praises of Israel. Our fathers trusted in thee: they trusted, and thou didst deliver them. They cried unto thee, and were delivered: they trusted in thee, and were not confounded. But I am a worm, and no man; a reproach of men, and despised of the people. All they that see me laugh me to scorn: they shoot out the lip, they shake the head saying, He trusted on the Lord that he would deliver him: let him deliver him, seeing he delighted in him. But thou art he that took me out of the womb: thou didst make me hope when I was upon my mother's breasts. I was cast upon thee from the womb: thou art my God from my mother's belly. Be not far from me; for trouble is near; for there is none to help. Many bulls have compassed me: strong bulls of Bashan have beset me round. They gaped upon me with their mouths, as a ravening and a roaring lion. I am poured out like water, and all my bones are out of joint: my heart is like wax; it is melted in the midst of my bowels. My strength is dried up like a potsherd; and my tongue cleaveth to my jaws; and thou hast brought me into the dust of death. For dogs have compassed me: the assembly of the wicked have enclosed me: they pierced my hands and my feet. I may tell all my bones: they look and stare upon me. They part my garments among them, and cast lots upon my vesture. But be not thou far from me, O Lord: O my strength, haste thee to help me. Deliver my soul from the sword; my darling from the power of the dog. I will declare thy name unto my brethren: in the midst of the congregation will I praise thee. Ye that fear the Lord, praise him; all ye the seed of Jacob, glorify him; and fear him, all ye the seed of Israel. For he hath not despised nor abhorred the affliction of the afflicted; neither hath he hid his face from him; but when he cried unto him, he heard. My praise shall be of thee in the great congregation: I will pay my vows before them that fear him. The meek shall eat and be satisfied: they shall praise the Lord that seek him: your heart shall live forever. All the ends of the world shall remember and turn unto the Lord:

and all the kindreds of the nations shall worship before thee. For the kingdom is the Lord's: and he is the governor among the nations. All they that be fat upon earth shall eat and worship: all they that go down to the dust shall bow before him: and none can keep alive his own soul. A seed shall serve him; it shall be accounted to the Lord for a generation. They shall come, and shall declare his righteousness unto a people that shall be born, that he hath done this."

"Wow!" I said. I looked at Margot. She nodded. I asked her, "Was that right, Margot?" Margot responded, "As far as what I can remember that was right on." I had Rachel quote some of the parts again. I was so stymied by her quotation that I just caught two or three phrases that sounded just like what we were facing. She was happy to. As amazing as it is for her to go from start to finish, it is even more astonishing that she can pick up where I ask, be stopped and go to another portion as I asked my questions! She said, "Actually, don't be too impressed. This was one I was learning when we were in hiding." She shared her story. Her family hid like many others, but could not stay that way as long as we had. It made me proud of Father.

I asked her about the passage where they took this man's clothing and gave it to others. We experienced that. Surrounded by dogs? We experienced that. We cry night and day for help, but get nothing. That was in her quotation. They mocked him for saying he belonged to God. They mock us too. He was a worm, despised by men. We are too. He was dry and thirsty. We are too. His bones were visible. There was so little skin and meat left on his ribs, that all of them could be counted. Ours are the same, as I looked down at my chest. They mocked him. They mock us. His heart melted. Ours are melting. The greatest part was what he said about how God had not left us. He has not despised us. What an encouragement that He is hearing our cries. He says that God will deliver and give life, and that we shall have food to eat. God is still the governor of all the earth, among the nations. The question always comes, "Who is this 'he'?"

Margot and I were satisfied. This was better than bread or meat. I told Rachel that I was amazed that King David faced so much of what we face. She agreed completely. She came back to what I said about this text being better than bread and meat. She said, "Jesus taught that man does not live on bread alone, but by every word that comes from the Mouth of God." What sustenance we had today. She also told me that the Christians apply this passage by David in his time of need as a prophecy pointing to the coming Messiah, Jesus. From what she read, it sure seemed to fit Jesus' sufferings too. It appears we are in the same boat as David and Jesus.

Tuesday, January 23, 1945

Dearest Kitty,

I have been thinking about a lot of things, off and on. I find myself repeating thoughts all day long. I can't seem to keep focus. Today is better. Rachel's quotations sure make me think about everything in my life today. Margot keeps trying to get up out of our bunk. I tried to get the Kapo to let us move her to the bottom bunk. The ladies below us were willing to switch, but she said no. I am so afraid Margot is going to hurt herself. She has dreams and tries to get up. When I leave her for a moment, she forgets she's sick and weak. In her lucid mind, she thinks her body should be intact too. She tries to get up, even gets to the point of hanging her feet off the bed, but her legs are like shoestrings. They hang straight down like they can hold her, only to fold when pressure is placed on them. Her whole body comes crashing down. Thankfully, we have been there each time to catch her. I can hardly leave her side. She is starting to get a rash.

My headaches are more painful and more frequent. I am shivering all the time. I don't know if it is because we are still at the door of our barrack, or if it is because I am getting sick too. We are seeing more and more hauled out of here. Elizabeth went today. I have a fever and I am wanting to throw up, but there is nothing in me to throw up. I know I must eat. They give us a little bread. I got a potato today, as did Margot. She would not eat it. I would not eat hers. I guarded it for her. Sadly, it sits under our blanket. I want to consume it, but I dare not. Maybe Margot will be able to eat it soon. We are allowed more water, but we have to go and get it. The guards are staying at a distance from us. Less of us here means a fraction more for us, but it is not enough to survive. The strongest do the lifting.

I haven't been to the fence in a few days. I haven't felt up to it. I am weak and I know that I must go get food. Where has my will gone? I will try to go tomorrow. I will just lay here today. Pray for me, Kitty.

Thursday, February 1, 1945

Dearest Kitty,

Margot is not doing well at all. I fear she is close to giving up. Even if she has the desire to continue, her body doesn't seem able. I am not much better than sister Margot. How sad for us both to be in this state. Is there anyone who will notice when we are gone? We had all these hopes and dreams. Yet, we lay here, literally dying. As I look around me, I realize the chances that Mother or Father have lived are miniscule at best. It would be a fluke if they are still alive. If they are, they are probably clinging to life by a single finger. Margot is hanging on by a pinky. I have about three fingers holding on, but two of them are slipping.

On a good note, Kitty, you are there listening to all that I am facing. On a surprising note, Mrs. Van Daan has been checking on us daily. She must realize our state. I am surprised by her concern. She has been sweet. She has brought us water. She has others check on us. I thought she would be the first to succumb to all this degradation, but she seems to have weathered it.

I was able to get a piece of bread today. I am so hungry. I ate it slowly hoping that the slower I ate it, the more it would satisfy. I tried to get Margot to drink a little water. I got some down her, but then she turned her head. I have not seen her open her eyes in days. She still can hear me. At times, she will roll to her side or back. We wait for some miracle to come.

Yours, Anne M. Frank

Monday, February 5, 1945

Dearest Kitty,

I was laying in bed around mid-afternoon and Mrs. Van Daan came to check on me and Margot. She brought me startling news. You will never believe this Kitty. Hanneli is alive, and she is here in this camp! I cannot believe it. I had all these dreams of her in torment, crying for my help. She was in so much pain. She was begging for me to get her out of Hell. I was haunted by this recurring dream. Many nights, I would see her in various stages of distress. I would try to help her in my dreams, but to no avail. Finally, when she would show her face in my dreams, and I was able, I would force myself awake. I could not bear it.

The only thing I could do was to pray for God to help her; to even bring her back to me. Have you ever prayed a prayer that you just knew was not possible? That was what I was praying for Hanneli. I was praying for God to be with her, and to help her, but I knew it was of no use. Then today, Ms. Van Daan says that Hanneli is alive and here in this camp and wants to see me! How good is our God, Kitty! He heard my prayers. If He can answer this prayer, can He not answer the prayer for Margot, or Father, or Mother, or even me?

I had to wait until dark before I could go to the fence. Mrs. Van Daan told me approximately where she had met Hanneli at the fence. I went as I was told. As I was walking to it, I heard my name, "Anne? Anne?" That was Hanneli's voice. It was unmistakable. Here is a girl that I went to school with. Here is the girl that I spent Jewish holidays with. Here is the girl whose parents were friends with my parents. Here's the girl who I spent many summer nights within their vacation house. We did so many things together. Just as it seems Margot is dying, God gives me Hanneli. How amazing! I answered, "Hanneli? Lies?" Her voice had not changed. I would know that voice anywhere. I grew up with it. I heard it in my dreams. I enjoyed it in my trips down memory lane. "Hanneli, it's you!" I said with joy. She said, "Yes Anne. It's me!"

I felt the flood of energy return, as well as tears of joy mixed with sadness. It is Hanneli, but we are here in Bergen-Belsen. We are enslaved together, but separated. Kitty, I began to cry. I have someone else to talk to who can talk back to me. I tried to hold it back, but I couldn't. I said, "Hanneli." I had so many things to tell her, but I could not quit crying. I broke down by the fence. I could not see her, nor could she see me. I put my hand against the straw that was laced between the barbs of the fence. I said, "Hanneli put your hand on the straw, third rung up of the barbed wire. Press against my hand please." She did. I cried. She cried. We could not speak. We didn't need to. There was consolation in her touch and in her presence.

Finally, she asked, "How did you get here, Anne? I thought you and your family had moved to Switzerland to avoid all this." I told her, "That was all a ruse to keep the Nazis from looking for us. I wish we would have been able to let your family know, but the Nazis came in on us too quickly. They had put a work summons out for Margot. Father had been expecting it and had built a hide-away for us in his warehouse. I am so sorry that we couldn't tell you. It all happened so suddenly. Please forgive us. There is no one I would rather have had with us than you and your family. We all grieved because of it. I had terrible dreams that you were dead, Hanneli. I felt so terrible because in the dreams, you kept asking why had I abandoned you. Please tell me how you got here? Is your family alive? Are they okay?"

Hanneli was so sweet. She said there was no hard feelings about not inviting them into our hiding place. Besides, we are all in the same predicament now. It would have made no difference. She told me that her mom, Mrs. Goslar, had died during childbirth and the baby died a few minutes later. How tragic. I had heard of the baby dying, but I had no idea that Mrs. Goslar died too. Lies said that she and her family had been picked up a year or so after we went into hiding. "The Germans blocked off our part of Amsterdam and went door to door looking for Jews. They got us in that round-up. We were sent to Westerbork." I told her, "We were sent there too at the end of 1944." She said they had been shipped out earlier that year to Bergen-Belsen. She said that her dad was in this camp, alive, but separated from her in another area during the day. They get together in the evenings. Her baby sister is with her, and they are staying in the same barrack. I was so happy to hear this news.

Hanneli told me that she heard things are a lot harsher where we are. She asked how were we doing and was my family safe and alive? I was sad to tell her that Father had been gassed when we arrived at Auschwitz. I paused when I told her that. It was the first time that I had ever said such a thing out loud. I was afraid to speak of it thinking that it might affect his fate. I cringed after I said it. Tears began to roll down my cheeks again. "Father was gassed. Father is dead. Father didn't make it out of Auschwitz. Father was killed when we arrived.." All those phrases echoed in my head. How can this be? How can I live? Hanneli noticed the silence, "Anne, are you there?" I told her, "I am sorry. That is the first time I have ever said that out loud to anyone. Mother is dead too. She was starving herself trying to feed us. She was getting weaker by the day. They shipped us here, but they left her behind. We have no misgivings about it. The only reason they kept Mother there was to gas her too.." What was I saying? It was all rolling out of my mouth like vomit. I was nauseated, but that wasn't literal vomit. It was more repulsive than that. What have these Germans done to my family. I am at the fence all alone.

I told Hanneli, "Father is dead. Mother is dead. I have no parents anymore, and I am not even sixteen years old. Margot is near death. I come to this fence, Lies, and I am the lone survivor. What have I to live for?" Hanneli picked up immediately, "Anne, you don't know for sure about your Mother. Margot may make it. My sister and I have been sick numerous times since we have been here, but we have made it. You will too. You have got to stay strong. You have always been strong, ever since I met you. You must live for them. You must live for me. I need you Anne. You have always been on my mind. It is so astounding that we have grown up together, studied together, and played together. It's only right that we suffer together, so that we can get through this together."

I was stirred by Hanneli's speech. I always admired her for speaking her mind. Maybe there is hope. Hanneli would not say it if she did not think it. She then asked me, "Is there anything I can do for you, Anne? We have it rough over on this side of the fence, but not near as rough as you on that side. We have our clothes. We get Red Cross packages. We are able to communicate somewhat with each other and help each other. Every day, some of our friends here throw food to your side.." I told her that I knew that was true. I had been the recipient of anonymous gifts before from her side. She asked me, "What do you need, Anne?" I told her, "Hanneli, I am so hungry. So is Margot. We have virtually nothing to eat. We get food perhaps every three or four days, but I don't want to take from you what you and your sister need. We don't have warm clothes. What we have are rags with holes. Do you remember my hair? How I loved my hair. They have shaved it off. I am nothing but stubble and bones." She said, "Come back in a few minutes. I have some food to share with you, my friend." I agreed to wait. I could not help but be thankful for this lifeline.

Hanneli returned. She had gathered some food from her pitiful stock, as well as from some of her friends. I was so moved. She had gone throughout her camp side, to her friends, gathering for me and Margot. Lots of people ask for food here, but no one gives it because it is like giving away a day of your life with each food morsel you share. These people were giving part of their lives, perhaps for me, a girl they didn't know. I was grateful beyond belief. I heard Hanneli's voice, "Are you ready, Anne?" I had not noticed that many women were at the fence waiting on anything to come over. I assumed they would wait for food to be thrown in their lane, and leave food thrown in my lane to me. I was terribly wrong. I told Hanneli with eyes of rescued expectation, "I'm ready." In silence, out of the blue, the package broke the plane of the fence. It was headed straight down to me. What a great throw! From the side, someone knocked me down. Two ladies grabbed the package and began to fight over it. They fell to the ground, rolling, shouting, "It's mine." The other said, "No, it's mine!" They were both wrong, it was mine! I began to scream as if my life was being squeezed out of me between a boat and a dock with me in between, helpless. I could not quit screaming with the loudest of cries. That was very dangerous, because we were not to be at the fence at night; much less, pass food over between us. I guess at that point I did not care. If my food is taken from me, they might as well kill me. My family is gone anyway.

Hanneli cried out, "What's wrong Anne? Didn't you get it?" By that time, the bigger woman had wrestled the package from the smaller woman and had run to her barrack. I told Hanneli in the most victimized tone, "A woman next to me took it. I chased after her, but she would not give it to me. What am I going to do?" I could not stop crying. I came out of my barrack with renewed hope. The stark reality snatched the little new-found hope I had. Hanneli consoled me when I returned, "Anne, it's okay. In a few more days, we will be getting another package. I will try again. We will be smarter next time. You will see." That was sweet of Lies and gentle. What she didn't understand was, I might not have a few more days. I thanked her. I told her that I would love to visit with her again tomorrow if we can. I am all alone. We agreed to meet at the same time tomorrow night. I am simply devastated, but too tired to weep any more.

Yours, Anne M. Frank

Tuesday, February 6, 1945

Dearest Kitty,

I spent the most of today caring for Margot. She won't drink hardly any water. I keep telling her that she needs it to survive. One of my bunk-mates reminded me that I needed it too. She said that I will not be able to take care of my sister if I don't take care of myself. She was right. The guards have pulled back on our duties. It seems thousands of us are sick. For certain, hundreds are dying each day. They carried twenty-three out of our barrack today. The body squad continues to carry the dead to the pit. I noticed that there are guards down by the pit digging. These aren't normal guards. They must be some soldiers who have been assigned this duty due to their cowardice in battle. Even though they are digging throughout the daylight hours, I glanced their way today and saw piles of bodies higher than the dirt enclosure. It won't be long until the whole camp is transported from the barracks to the pit by wheelbarrow. The last to die will probably be left in the wheelbarrows with no one to empty them into the pit.

Let's change the subject. What a joy it is to have old friends reunited. I looked forward all day to visiting with Hanneli. I met her tonight at our usual spot. I pray this is the second of many visits. My longing would be that we could be in the same barrack. I told her that. She agreed. She asked me what happened last night with that food parcel dropped from her side to mine. I told her, "I am still bitter about the lady taking my food. Had it not been that lady, it would have been the other. Technically, I am mad at both. Father always taught us to take care of our family, but to also take care of others. He showed us, by example, to care for people. He actually once said that we don't need as much as we have, and that we can live on less than we do. It was that premise that caused him to take people into our hiding place. We shared our food when no one else shared theirs. He never complained, though we did." Hanneli responded, "I loved your father. He was always so gracious and kind. My father was so wrapped up in the coming doom that it was hard to live a child's life growing up. Don't get me wrong, I love my father and would not trade him for anything. But, your father always brought a lift to ours." I told her how much it meant to hear her say that, "You are the only one I know, other than Margot, that I can have an honest, mutual conversation about Pim. I cannot visit with Mrs. Van Daan about him. In the back of my mind, I still see her flirting with him. I can't stand that thought and don't want her to go there in her mind." Hanneli really latched on to this and started laughing, "I cannot believe that! Mrs. Van Daan!" A lady on my side told us to hold it down. She said, "There is nothing to laugh about in this place!" I generally would agree, but for a few nights, we were just school girls gossiping. What a relief from the strain of destitution.

Hanneli than asked me, "Do you remember when we would drop water out of the window of your apartment on people down below?" I told her, "I sure do! Father is a great man, but if he ever caught us, you would have seen a different side. He would have been loving, but we would have regretted it dearly. If we were back there now, I would stand below and let you pour the water on me. I would open my mouth and drink as much as I could. Then I would take a bar of soap and a rag out there and get a good washing. You would be exhausted carrying all that water to the window!" She told me that we would have to take turns. We both need a good bath. She then asked me, "And, do you remember when we played hopscotch so hard that the earth quaked on the other side of the globe?" "That was so funny," I told her. "Our imaginations were creative even then!"

Time flew by. I wanted to stay, but I told her that I needed to get in and check on Margot. With that said, I told her that as much as Margot needed me to check on her, I needed Hanneli at this time. Hanneli told me she loved me. I told her the same. "Can we meet again tomorrow here?", I inquired hopefully. She responded, "I would not miss it! I have some questions for you about our growing up." I proudly proclaimed, "It's a deal."

Thank You, God, for our friends!

Yours, Anne

Wednesday, February 7, 1945

Dearest Kitty,

I feel so much better on the inside. I don't think I am getting better physically, but if our spirits are lifted up, will our bodies not follow? I tended to Margot. I was able to get a change of clothes for her. She had been rotating between freezing and sweating all night. She is hallucinating. She points to the wall of our barrack and tells me there's a hole in the wall, "Look at it, Anne. Do you see it?" I would tell her, "No, Margot, there is no hole there." She would get angry and curse me. That has never

ever happened before. Margot never cursed except to mock someone or to quote someone in their indiscretion. Mother never liked a curse word said, or hear one repeated. Now, I hear more bad words from my sister. She is awake and unsettled. She wants to get up, but I have to hold her down. She keeps coming back to the hole in the wall, "Anne, there's food in that hole. Izzo has hid it there for us. Get it for us please. There is enough for both of us." I go to the wall, rub the plaster and say, "See Margot, there is no hole there. I have some bread in our blanket." I walked over, climbed up into our bunk, and handed it to her. She looked at me with a broken heart, "You are my sister, Anne. I thought you loved me, but you won't even give me the food that Izzo has left for me. Why do you hate me?" I just wanted to cry, "Margot, I love you. I would never keep anything from you." She kept demanding it, so I got back down and went to the wall. I pretended to put my hand in an imaginary hole and came back to her with a palm out to her. I said, "I found it Margot. Here it is. You were right, there is bread and potatoes, too." She looked in my hand, but never reached. She closed her eyes to sleep. Pacified, I hope.

I could not meet Hanneli at the fence, but I told another lady here where I would meet her each night. She told her that I would be there tomorrow night. How sad I was to have to stay in. It was my only bright spot of each dreary day. I was a prisoner in my barrack. I was a captive on the grounds. I was a caged animal when I ate. But, when I went to the fence, I was a girl again with friends, family, and stories to tell. Sacrifice. That is what love is. Father sacrificed for us. Mother sacrificed for us too. Now, I am sacrificing for Margot. I pray Heaven records these things. Otherwise, no one will ever know. We will have been born, lived, and died with no one ever knowing an Anne Frank was here.

Yours, Anne M. Frank

Thursday February 8, 1945

Dearest Kitty,

I had a restless night sleeping; or should I say, Margot had a restless night sleeping. Thus, I had little or no sleep at all. I could use some good news. I made it through the day longing for my meeting at the fence with Hanneli. Strange, when I was in the Annexe, I felt she needed me. Now, we are together, and I find that I need her. I wonder if she needs any help at all. She seems so stable. She is in the same prison I am, but she has her needs somewhat met. She is not desperate. She is not crying out. She has her father and sister. From what I can tell, they are both healthy. She has not lost a family member here. Her mother died, but that was of natural causes in childbirth. She seems strong, though I cannot see her. She may look the same as me or worse. I won't know unless the dividing wall between us is lifted.

I got to the wall early. What great news I heard! She said, "I have your doll." I was confused. Margot was not making sense, but not Hanneli too? I asked, "My doll?" She said, "Yes, you know I tried to get a doll to you earlier but someone stole it?" I knew now what she meant, "Oh Hanneli, thank you for the doll! How can I get it?" The women around us looked confused. Hanneli said, "Let's go near the guard tower, by the last barrack in the shadow." I assumed the barracks on our side were parallel to those on her side. She had been here longer, so I figured she knew best. The great thing about this location was that no other prisoner risked being that close to the guard tower. We had to talk lower. Hanneli asked, "Is anyone around you?" I told her, "No." She said with a release, "Here comes your doll." The guard was looking into the field, smoking his usual cigarette. I looked his way as it was in midair, and it was safe. I caught it, clutched it, and put it under my rag of a dress, "Oh thank you Hanneli. Thank you!" She said, "Don't mention it. Take it back to your barrack so no one can get it. Eat what you can. Give some to Margot. I will meet you at our normal place tomorrow." Delighted, I said goodbye and walked as briskly as I could to my barrack, climbed up into the middle bunk next to Margot and opened our delicacies.

When you are hungry, anything is good. That was the case tonight. I think what made it better was that it was from someone who was my friend; from someone who loved me. It's like when Mother would make my favorite homemade cookies and slide them into my lunch sack, beneath the napkin the night before without me knowing. I would get to school, open my sandwich and visit with my friends. I would eat my fruit, which I loved. I then would grab my napkin to wipe my mouth. There it would be: my surprise all wrapped up. A little sugary discus of love. It was super special. This food tonight meets that criteria.

Yours, Anne

Friday, February 9, 1945

My dearest Kitty,

I saved some of the food from Hanneli for Margot, but she would not eat. I tried to tell her about Hanneli, but I don't think she understood me. She just lays there breathing. When I am awake, she sleeps. When I try to sleep, she won't quit fighting some unseen battle. I am famished for food, though Hanneli is helping. I am desperate for rest, but Margot isn't helping. That's not a problem. This is what love looks like. I have never had the chance to really care for anyone. When Grandmother was ill, I was able to help a little, but Mother carried most of the load. This is the first time I have had the opportunity to help someone who really needed it, while at the same time show a loved one how much I love them. Hanneli is doing the same for me.

I met Hanneli at the fence tonight. We talked about old times. We even dared to talk about times when we get out of here. We talked about her family's devotion to our faith. They were in synagogue every Sabbath. They observed every Jewish holiday to the letter. I loved to be with them during the Feast of Tabernacles. She loved to be with us during Yom Kippur so she could eat instead of fast. Hanneli then came to a question she said she had been meaning to ask me. I told her, "Ask it. I am an open book!" She asked me, "Why was your family not religious?" I was surprised by the question, "Lies, we were and are very religious. What makes you think we weren't?" She said, "Your family seldom came to synagogue. Your family never observed a Jewish holiday in your home that I can remember. You came to our home at some of them, but for the most part your mother and father were non-participants." I said, "Margot and Mother were at synagogue pretty often." Hanneli said, "Yes, they did go from time to time, but it seemed they came as observers."

This was something that I had to think about for a minute. The time in my head to think seems a lot longer than the physical pause to speak. I said, "Hanneli, I can understand why you think that. In the ritualistic sense of organized Judaism, my parents were slack. But, in our home, I have never seen a more religious couple, faithful to God. Every night, we said our prayers. Every day, we were to read the Torah, Poetry, and Prophets. Beyond this, we observed the religious holidays, but more at home as a family in private. We observed Hanukkah and other Jewish holidays at home. We also celebrated St. Nicholas Day and Christmas." Hanneli said, "I had no idea Anne. That is great! I love knowing that your family took our culture and faith so personally." I assured her we did. I did not want her to think I was just trying to put up a defense. Hanneli and I had several things in common; one of them speaking our mind. We visited a little more after that. She had other questions, but not as serious as that one. I thanked her so much for the package. As usual, we expectantly planned to visit the next day.

I came back to our bunk and checked on Margot, where I now lay. Hanneli really made me wonder about my family's faith. Thinking back, our faith was practiced in our home, in the Annexe, in Westerbork, and then Auschwitz without Father. We have continued in our observance here in Bergen-Belsen, without either Mother or Father. Our practice of faith has always been daily, steady, and sincere. I remembered the dream I had about Hanneli, and how I feared that she didn't know the Lord. My longing was that I would have told her more about God and made sure that she was in relationship with Him. I knew she was religious, but my fear was it was forced upon her, and that it was a ritual only. Tonight, I was so wrapped up in defending our religious lives that I did not ask her if she truly has a relationship with God. Why do I keep missing my opportunities?

Pim was faithful to pray with us and to make sure we were praying. He wanted us to know God's Word and to put it into practice. This is where I have great confidence in knowing where Father is. His works showed us that his faith in God was real. He loved people, cared for them, was totally honest in business, took care of his family, and his own mother. He helped his family when they were in need, putting his own ambitions on hold. He was forgiving and longsuffering. He lived as God would have him live. He has taught us the same. The Goslars may struggle with his participation in Christmas. I think Pim had some questions about Jesus and His ties to the Old Testament prophets. He asked the question I think every Jewish man or woman should ask. Where is the Messiah? When will He come? Will He come? Did He come already, and we didn't recognize Him?

I know where I stand. I know where Margot and Mother stand too. This gives me great comfort, win or lose, live or die.

Yours, Anne

ANNE'S DEPARTURE

Dearest Kitty,

I have not been well. Margot has been worse. I made it to the fence once. I told Hanneli that I could not stay long. I was able to ask her about her relationship with God. I asked her, "Did you go to synagogue and observe holidays because you are Jewish, because your parents did, or because you really love and want to please God?" She tried to explain it to me as she reasoned in her mind the answer. I felt a deep sense of searching in her heart. She was so sincere. I was greatly comforted by her answer. Truly, the answer to that question is such that no outward answer will suffice. It is all bound to the decision a person sincerely makes on the inside. I am so glad I asked her. I told her that I looked forward to our visit the next evening when hopefully I would feel better. Sadly, I have not been feeling better.

Yours, Anne

Sunday, February 18, 1945

Dearest Kit,

I can hardly get out of bed. Mrs. Van Daan is bringing us water and a little bread with the help of some of our other bunkmates. I wonder if they are afraid to be near us. Others are, but then again, there is nowhere to go to escape our sickness. It is in every barrack, lurking at every bunk. It has crawled up into our middle bunk, laid on top of us, enveloped us, and then melted into our bodies.

Everything I have seen Margot go through, now I am going through, except for the hallucinations. But, how can I say that? Do I know when I am hallucinating? This is the roughest sickness I have ever felt. Every centimeter of my body hurts. Every organ labors. I have a rash now on my body to add to my misery.

Friday, February 23, 1945

My darling Kitty,

I have been asleep now for a while. I was just awakened with someone pouring water into my mouth. I turned my head to spit it out. I was not expecting that. I was choking, but after some coughs, I was able to clear my airway. I have no idea what is going on around me. Is the war over? Did we win? Where is Mother? Is Father out of town? Tell Margot to quit hitting me.

Hello, Kitty! Hand me my diary please. It's under the table. Tell Dussel I need my turn at the desk. Look at the roses Peter brought me. Aren't they pretty! He is so sweet.

Monday, February 26, 1945

My dearest Kitty,

I felt a little better this morning. I was able to sit up. I noticed Margot was not by my side. I asked if she was better? Mrs. Van Daan said she would be alright. There was something about her tone that told me she was not telling the truth. She never could lie very well. I asked Rachel, who was there to dab my forehead with part of her sleeve, "Rachel, she's dead, isn't she?" Without hesitation, but in a gentle voice, she said, "Yes, Anne. She's no longer suffering." I opened my eyes wide and tried to focus, "What happened?" Rachel said she tried to get out of bed, fell, and hit her head on the bunk beside ours. I began to cry. I closed my eyes and wished to join her, Father, and Mother. I want us to be a family again.

Tuesday, February, 27, 1945

My dearest Kitty,

I awoke this morning with more ladies around me. Mrs. Van Daan was there. She told me that Hanneli says, hello, and wanted to remind me that today is Purim. Purim? What does that mean? I cannot remember. Wait, I do remember. "It is our Jewish holiday to observe the day that we were rescued from destruction. Someone had wanted to kill us." I looked up, "Is that right, Rachel?" She said, "Yes, we were rescued from that wicked man, Haman. It was in the evilest of times that the steel of Esther and Mordecai shown the brightest as recorded in the Book of Esther. God is mentioned nowhere in that Book, which is odd for the Old Testament writings, but all through the Book, God's Hand is seen busily at work." I thought to myself, "How I want to be steeled, but I fear it is too late. There is nothing left to steel."

She continued, "It is at this time that we celebrate that we as a people were delivered from extinction." Now I remember. I took a drink and laid back. I said nothing, but I am thinking. Kitty, how appropriate is Purim now. I feel as though I am living in that day. I feel history continues to repeat itself and always will. Evil against Good. Satan against God. The world against the Jews. This place against me. Our lives hang in the balance of this struggle. I am so weak right now, I feel for certain that we will lose as a people unless an Esther and a Mordecai rise up. Who will that be? Eisenhower and Churchill? The Americans, the British, and the Russians? Our people were delivered just in time, at their point of extinction. Will we be rescued just in time? Will I be? Will there be anything left of me? I am sure Margot lays outside our barrack, cold and stiff, eyes wide open, and gaunt, but she is at peace.

We don't see God anywhere in this. In fact, many here are Jewish who have renounced that there is a God. They say if He exists, why are we going through this? They asked the same in Egypt. They asked the same in Jerusalem as the Romans burned the Temple. They asked the same in Gamla as men and women leaped to their deaths. But God was working. He was there. Because He was there, the Jewish people are still here. I believe we will always be. God cannot let His chosen people be eradicated because He promised. And, if His Promises aren't kept, then His Throne cannot continue.

So, I ask the question again, where is our Esther or our Mordecai? We are nearing the time of Passover, and as I wait, where is our Elijah to announce the coming of our Messiah? I can hardly hold my head up now. My parents are dead. How could I surmise any other outcome? My sister is dead. My breath grows faint. My heart has a sharp pain that makes it hard for me to breathe. The ladies around me rub my arm. Another kisses my forehead. I hurt so bad. I am not even wanting food any more. It hurts so. I am able to whisper, "I don't want to fight anymore." A woman says, "You don't have to."

For some reason Kitty, I think the fight is over for me. Where is our Deliverer, the Messiah? Or, has He come? I am falling to sleep now, my darling Kitty. I believe He has come. And, He has come for me. *Auf wiederhoren*. Until we speak again.

THE LAST CHAPTER

In February or March, 1945, a day after Margot's battle ended, Anne Frank's ended too. Their Mother died of starvation in Auschwitz approximately a month before. Much to their surprise, her Father Otto lived through Auschwitz and was liberated when the Russians entered their camp. It is because of Otto Frank and Miep Gies that the world is blessed with their story.

Edith Frank's body was most likely taken to the crematorium and disposed of as irreverently and unnoticed as millions before in that camp. Margot and Anne's bodies were thrown into the pit at Bergen-Belsen and buried in a mass grave, much like millions more across Europe.

Unlike the others, there is a written record of Anne to go with the oral and photographic record shared by her father and friends. Anne died perhaps thinking she would be like the nameless, faceless others who were forgotten by a world that didn't seem to care. The beauty of Anne's story is that her dreams were accomplished beyond what she could have ever hoped or dreamed. She did become a famous writer, and her life has changed the world for the better.

What is known of Anne Frank is an honest, imperfect life. She struggled with fears, emotions, and temptations like every other person. She had lessons to learn and things she wished she could take back. She hoped for the best of mankind and sometimes saw it. Other times, she was greatly disappointed. She grappled with realities – physical, mental, and spiritual. This is the course of every person born. The difference, most likely, is that very few are recorded in such a sobering and raw way.

In this companion to her diary, Anne saw the bodies of those victimized and wanted to tell their story. She knew each had a story, but sadly there was no one to record it and tell it. That is what a journalist would do. Anne would have done it if she had been given the chance. Even her story was not completely told. It can only be speculated on based on the surrounding facts.

There is a harsh wall that each life must hit. Even the most famous are remembered but for a few generations. Time pushes each life into an unmarked grave. The hardness of life and the certainty of death causes each to question the purpose of this thing given called life.

That is the question and the answer. Life is given. It is given for a reason and Anne saw this. She felt the need for every life to be recorded, especially hers. Every human being wants life recorded, especially theirs. Thankfully, there is One who records each life. It has to be so; otherwise, there would be no unique fingerprint or individual DNA marker to put with each story.

But, what good is it to have it recorded if death comes, and that is the end? To be remembered is no satisfaction to one who can no longer think or feel. It is only in heading to death, that anyone is concerned about being remembered. Once the death line is crossed, it no longer matters; unless? Anne knew there is an eternal life and an eternal death. The record of each life determines the impact and the destination that follows. This makes the record of a life even more important. Records can only be changed in the now, while living. Anne knew it was imperative for Izzo to change while he still could. She longed for Peter Van Daan to change so he could be all that he should. In her diary, she grieved over not having made sure Hanneli had a relationship with God before it was too late.

The more Anne wanted her Mother to change, the more Anne realized she herself needed to change. It was her prayer, her longing in her diary and it can be no doubt her striving after the last entry was made. Mankind rejoices at how Anne Frank affected this world for the better. May mankind learn from what she saw and faced, and respond in a way that she would desire. May the readers of this work strive to change and affect this world in the same way, no matter what challenges they face, knowing their lives affect others. That effect is recorded. That record is rewarded. Because of this, every story can have a good ending.

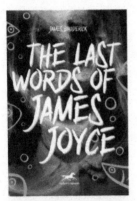

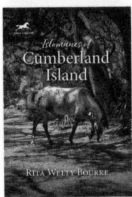